FROM THIS DAY FORWARD

JOHN BRUNNER

From This Day
Forward

Doubleday & Company, Inc.

Garden City, New York

All stories included herein have been specially revised by the author for book publication.

Acknowledgments:
THE BIGGEST GAME first appeared in *Science Fantasy*, copyright © 1955 by Nova Publications and (under the title THE MEN IN BLACK) in *Startling Mystery Stories*, copyright © 1966 by Health Knowledge Inc.
THE TROUBLE I SEE first appeared in *New Worlds*, copyright © 1959 by Nova Publications.
AN ELIXIR FOR THE EMPEROR first appeared in *Fantastic*, copyright © 1964 by Ziff-Davis Publishing Company.
WASTED ON THE YOUNG first appeared in *Galaxy*, copyright © 1965 by Galaxy Publishing Corp.
EVEN CHANCE first appeared in *Analog*, copyright © 1965 by The Condé Nast Publications Inc.
PLANETFALL first appeared in *Analog*, copyright © 1965 by The Condé Nast Publications Inc.
JUDAS first appeared in *Dangerous Visions*, edited by Harlan Ellison, copyright © 1967 by Harlan Ellison.
THE VITANULS first appeared in *The Magazine of Fantasy & Science Fiction*, copyright © 1967 by Mercury Press Inc.
FACTSHEET SIX first appeared in *Galaxy*, copyright © 1968 by Galaxy Publishing Corp.
FIFTH COMMANDMENT first appeared in *Vision of Tomorrow*, copyright © 1970 by Ronald E. Graham.
FAIRY TALE first appeared in *Vision of Tomorrow*, copyright © 1970 by Ronald E. Graham.
THE INCEPTION OF THE EPOCH OF MRS. BEDONEBYASYOU-DID first appeared in *Quark*, copyright © 1971 by Coronet Communications.
THE OLDEST GLASS, copyright © 1972 by Brunner Fact & Fiction Ltd.

CONTENTS

A "FROM THIS DAY FOREWORD," AS IT WERE

It behooves us all to be interested in the future, because that's where we're going to spend the rest of our lives.

I wish I knew who said that! I wish I didn't know so many people who aren't listening to it! For it has been said, equally aptly, *Blessed are they who expect the worst, for they shall get it.*

All these stories are about people—individuals or groups —to whom, very suddenly, *the* future happens. The future that closes like the jaws of a trap . . . or the one which lays down a path to follow that it's no longer possible to avoid . . . or which merely maps a life coloured with hopeless resignation.

The future is waiting in ambush. And the location of that ambush?

Why—today!

JKHB

FROM THIS DAY FORWARD

THE BIGGEST GAME

The first time Royston noticed one of the men in black was as he paused before entering the gym. The door of the gym was a big mirror; across the middle of it gilt letters asked, SATISFIED? and a foot below that it said, COME IN!

Royston was going in. He was one of the customers who came here because he was satisfied with himself, and meant to stay that way. He was more preening before the glass than actually examining his body. He'd learned how to exploit his magnificent physique and leonine blond hair when he was about fifteen. Now, at forty, he looked as well as he felt—terrific.

He smiled. Perfect even teeth showed in his reflected face. He cocked his head to judge the effect, and the movement brought the man in black into the corner of the mirror.

Royston froze.

The man was just standing there, watching him—not doing anything. His face was as blank as a wax dummy's. Nonetheless Royston was embarrassed at having been caught openly admiring himself. Hastily he pushed at the door and entered the gym.

He'd forgotten the man in black well before the end of his hour-long workout. He enjoyed the atmosphere of this place so much that nothing could have distracted him. He knew—the masseurs and coaches had often told him—that just about every other customer of his age who came here did so in order to sweat off a pot belly or wear down a seat swollen with chair-polishing. Royston came to keep the shape and muscle-tone he'd had at twenty, and he was doing fine.

There was a bunch of pansies in today, from a theatre up the street with a big new musical in rehearsal, and a couple of them started hanging around him. A word from one of the coaches, however, sent them back to their buddies with disappointed faces. Royston grinned. It was two years since one of that sort had really bothered him. That time he'd been so disgusted he'd let the boy catch him alone in the changing-room—and broken his nose for him.

Since then, the coaches automatically warned them off.

Not that he minded them staring at him enviously, of course; envy even from that source set him up for the day. When he left—healthily relaxed, cleansed by a shower, his deodorant renewed—he was humming to himself.

But as the mirrored door swung shut behind him he stopped in his tracks. The man in black was still there, watching him.

Correction: not specifically watching *him*, but giving a quick once-over to each of the passers-by, as if waiting for an acquaintance whose face he didn't remember clearly. His expression, as before, was an absolute blank.

Royston shrugged. Well, if the guy had friends who stood him up for a solid hour that was his worry. He caught sight of an approaching cab and hailed it with a shout. There were more important matters to consider.

He pondered them during a pleasant afternoon alone in his apartment. He reached his decision while pulling through his .255 Mannlicher, and worked out the details of what he must do to implement it while putting some clear lacquer on the newly polished barrel of an elderly jezail. Nothing was further from his mind than men in black when he left home for his crucial date of that evening.

Until he saw that a man in black, with a face of complete vacuity, was sauntering along the road not far away.

Instantly he was alert. In his chosen way of life he had long ago learned not to dismiss such events as coincidental. He had meant to hail a cab as soon as possible; instead he took to the busy underground and went four stations in the wrong direction before emerging to locate one. Through its rear window he kept a watchful eye on any vehicle which might be following his, and—just in case—got out two blocks distant from Lulabelle's home.

There was no one suspicious in sight. Maybe it had been coincidence after all.

Of course his detour meant that he was late arriving —but in view of the decision he had come to earlier, that was the reverse of a drawback.

Lulabelle was twenty-four and extremely pretty. She was married to a man only a few years older who obviously knew hardly anything about women. His family had settled a small fortune on him when he married, since which time he had apparently acted under the impression that if he gave his wife enough cash she wouldn't want anything else. Royston, whose face was his fortune, knew better and had exploited that knowledge.

In fact, the only thing wrong with Lulabelle was that her husband was due back from his business trip to Japan in one week's time, and Royston's regular deadline for withdrawal from a compromising situation was seven days.

He had been tempted to put off the fatal moment. Lulabelle had accumulated a good deal of frustrated passion since her wedding day, and moreover she was of a generous disposition. Still, there were plenty of women in the world, and his habit of leaving himself several days to disengage had always saved him from unnecessary complications.

With a slight pang of regret he set his plan in motion. Over dinner he bored her by telling her a story about a man-eating leopard. He told it very well, considering it wasn't true, but she had heard it before almost word for word. Later he was cooler than usual, and pretended not to be paying attention while she retailed some gossip to him—in fact he took it in with care, of course, because scandal was always useful, but he made sure his eyes were wandering and his comments were random ones, polite but empty.

It worked. It always worked. Hurt and puzzled, Lulabelle pleaded tiredness when he took her home from the restaurant where they had eaten, and refused to let him come in. That too was according to plan—it was a reflexive response, the withholding of sexual privileges on a basis of "See what you're cheating yourself out of!"

He was standing on the front steps of her apartment block trying to persuade himself that the proceeds from a gold cigarette lighter, cuff-links, a jade statuette and sundry other recent presents was a fair recompense for his self-denial, when he saw that a man in black was standing across the street, his face as impassive as a wall.

A chill trembled down his spine, and he concluded that his early night was a very good idea.

The next morning was bright and sunny, but he woke to it in a black mood. Lulabelle must be put out of his life as of last night, and no qualifications. That would teach him to break his customary rule about living spouses. Japan was a long way off, but rumours of infidelity seemed to reach suspicious husbands, regardless of where they might be, as surely as though they had been relayed by satellite.

Time to go hunting again, then, and this time for a prey less dicey than Lulabelle.

He thought with nostalgia of Moira Parmenter, the widow who had set his standards for him ten years ago. He shook his head over the recollection of her suicide. Such a pity! It could have been avoided if he'd perfected his technique for letting women down gently a year or two sooner. Now he had nothing to remember her by at all; the Mercedes convertible, the matched pair of Purdey guns, everything had gone the way of all fleshpots.

And the bitch didn't even alter her will in my favour first!

Still, even if the Moira Parmenters of this world were exceptional, the species she typified was common enough.

He ate breakfast with a book on tiger-shooting open beside his plate. His African background had been reliable for a long time, and he could expertly intersperse his yarns of adventure on the veld with hair-raising examples of how the stupid blacks were letting their countries go to rack and ruin, but recently he had picked up a fine tiger skin, too good to waste, and there were no tigers in Africa.

Once or twice he had thought of going on safari in reality. A long time ago he had actually made plans for such a trip. Then someone came up and he had to postpone it, and when he was next in a position to afford the outlay the idea didn't seem so attractive—scorching sun, insect bites, a diet of biltong and canned beans . . . So the Mannlicher and the .455 elephant gun and the

rest stayed on the wall, and the hunter remained content with his chosen prey.

For—and he chuckled as he stowed the book about
tigers next to his leather-bound volumes of Rowland
Ward game records—wasn't he the big game hunter *par
excellence?* What game could compare with a human
quarry?

He had trophies aplenty on his walls which he claimed
to have won, but had not; in his bank account, though,
there were others of a different kind which he had. And
there was danger in his hunting, too—several times he
had himself become the hunted, stalked by private detectives and angry husbands. He laughed at the recollection of how often he had fooled them, then grew
suddenly grave.

Did he have a case of the same thing on his hands at
the moment, with these men in black who had three times
so far turned up at the same spot as himself? It wasn't
likely; they didn't behave like any detectives who had
followed him before, and they seemed to make no effort
to conceal their presence. Suppose, however, the husband
was unwilling to believe in his wife's adultery, or eager
to avoid a fuss about it, and had merely instructed them
to warn off this man who was setting siege to her . . . ?

He shrugged. The only sensible course at the moment
was to begin a round of innocent activities and see what
happened. He was due for a visit to the barber. That
would be a suitable first step.

He was shaken rigid when he rose from the barber's
chair and dusted the last hair-clippings from his neck
with the towel he was obsequiously handed. Turning
towards the street window of the shop, he discovered a
man in black gazing expressionlessly at him.

Making no attempt to disguise his interest, he remained there while Royston paid up, put his coat on and left the shop.

This is too much!

Royston set his lips in a narrow line and turned along the street. At random he paused to study the window display of an oculist—something he would normally have avoided by instinct, for the threat of having to wear glasses was a recurrent nightmare and his eyes were too sensitive for contact lenses.

The man in black had followed him, and had now halted and was blatantly waiting for him to move on.

That settled it. His plan for letting Lulabelle down gently was shot to blazes, and he was going to have to take the chance of her suffering an attack of conscience and confessing to her husband. With these men in black trailing him, obviously to frighten him off since they were so open about staring at him, he wasn't going to call her up, let alone go near her home. Logically the end-result of the process which had been set in motion was not meant to be a divorce suit. More likely it would be a razor slash, or vitriol.

In a very grim mood he turned into a convenient restaurant for lunch.

The mood lightened miraculously. He had been sitting at his table a mere ten minutes, with the restaurant growing more and more crowded, when he saw approaching someone who alerted all his professional instincts.

A mature woman, to put it kindly. Pearls, very probably genuine uncultured. Slipping real mink off her shoulders as the headwaiter deferentially guided her past his table. It was the work of a moment to organise a gentle trip, and a flurry of apology, and a series of concerned inquiries as to whether she was hurt . . . and an invitation to share his table by way of recompense for the inadvertent offence he had given her.

Almost hungrily—in the spiritual rather than the physical sense—she accepted the proposal.

The more he looked her over, the more convinced he became that she was a gift from Providence. Her face was still quite pretty, but promisingly vapid and made up with a kind of anxious thoroughness. Her clothes had cost a great deal but she hadn't been able to buy the talent to wear them successfully. In short, she had every trait of the kind of woman he could tie around his finger.

He rose to her bait with the most dazzling smile he had achieved in weeks, guided her through the menu and wine-list and chose a meal for her which was already spiced with flattery before it was served. He introduced himself; he steered the conversation around to the romance of travel; he improvised a story which put the recently acquired tiger skin to excellent use.

She didn't contribute much to the conversation, but what she did have to say was music to his ears. Her name was Mrs. Arnheim and she was divorced from someone in plastics. She was wallowing in alimony. The divorce was more than a year in the past and she was lonely. Travel to her had nothing to do with romance— it implied taking a cruise on which there were ten women for every man. And so forth. Faced with a situation like this, Royston could hardly compare himself to a big game hunter. He felt more like the general who was awoken at two in the morning by a frantic aide reporting that the country was being invaded, who said, "Look in Drawer B," and went back to sleep.

He paid for her lunch with good grace. He never begrudged a small investment in an undertaking that was guaranteed to repay dividends.

When he was helping her into a cab afterwards, she

laid a bejewelled hand on his arm, called him *dear* Mr. Royston, and looked several invitations at him. He leafed rapidly through a mental index, settled on dinner as the next step, and made a date.

That evening his phone rang several times. He let it ring. There was a man in black across the street, who stood for more than an hour clearly visible under a lamp before he moved away.

His first outing with Mrs. Arnheim was not the unqualified success he had expected. There was a man in black at the adjacent table in the restaurant, sitting alone and eating with a kind of machinelike absent-mindedness. He had nothing in common with the other men in black apart from the colour of his clothes, a general similarity of build and the lack of expression on his face. Nonetheless Royston found himself automatically thinking that this was the first time he had seen one of *them* do anything but stand and stare.

It was his turn to do the staring. The man seemed to be consuming his food in a trance. He appeared to be chewing to a regular count—so many movements of the jaw up and down, with a rhythm as inflexible as a metronome's, swallow, re-load and chew again, the tempo bearing no relation to what had been on his fork.

Royston berated himself silently. Looking at the matter in objective terms, what evidence did he have that all these men in black were associated? At any given moment there might be thousands of men in black suits on the streets of London. Perhaps having his self-esteem piqued by the one who had caught him admiring his own reflection had made him subconsciously more sensitive to their presence. In any case, he was going to steer clear religiously from Lulabelle, and if he stuck to that decision he would have nothing to worry about.

He snatched his attention back to Mrs. Arnheim, and had the biggest shock of his life when he discovered that she also was eating in that strange mechanical fashion.

What was going on? Had someone revived that health fad about chewing every mouthful forty-three times, or whatever the number was? He almost demanded an explanation, but caught himself in time. Personal matters were not yet on that programme for ensnaring Mrs. Arnheim.

He fixed a date for a theatre the following night, and took her home in a mood even bleaker than yesterday's, though he disguised it under a veneer of practised charm. When he got out of his own cab in front of his apartment a short time later he was expecting to find another of the men in black somewhere nearby. He was right. In the same place as last night, at the edge of the pool of brightness cast by a streetlamp.

Abruptly his patience snapped. Telling the cabby to wait a second, he strode over to the silent watcher.

And halted.

He hadn't been as right as he'd thought. This wasn't *another* of the men in black. It was the same one who had been in the restaurant an hour ago.

"Hey, you!" Royston snapped. "What's the idea of following me around?"

The man stirred and half turned to confront him. For one horrible instant Royston had the impression that his face was melting, like wax in a flame. Then the man spoke, his voice as neutral as his features.

"Following you, sir? You must be mistaken."

And the face was not that of the man in the restaurant.

Royston felt his jaw drop. What was this—a hallucination? A trick of the light? Conscience deceiving him into thinking that any man wearing black was pursuing him? The word *paranoia* loomed up in his mind.

Muttering a frantic apology, he returned with his palms sweating to pay off his cab. When he looked around from the entrance of the apartment block the man in black was nowhere to be seen.

He had to take several stiff shots of brandy before he could sleep, and then he dreamed of being haunted by black figures without faces.

The next day, however, there were no men in black anywhere to be seen. Gradually he began to think of last night's shock as mere illusion, a product of anxiety which would not recur. He cheered up considerably, and his evening with Mrs. Arnheim at the theatre was a roaring success in consequence. He wasn't sure of the fact until he had escorted her home; she seldom showed much expression because she was apparently unable to stop worrying about what moving her face might do to her elaborate makeup. But as he accompanied her to her door she did crack a recognisable smile and ask if he would care to come in for a nightcap.

He would.

It was almost too pat. Her maid, she told him, had been instructed to go to bed, which made it easy for him to take charge, settle her on a sofa and attend to the drinks —from a cabinet so well stocked a hotel bar would not have been ashamed of the range. The momentary separation gave him his first opportunity to appraise the furniture, the decorations, the pictures and the ornaments. No doubt about it: this place spelled MONEY in letters of fire. Properly handled, Mrs. Arnheim could well become a second Moira Parmenter—and this time there wouldn't be any nonsense about suicide before the will was amended.

He found some light music on the radio, took his place beside her on a sofa, and plied her with his best line of

late-night conversation. Compliments in abundance, naturally—mostly concerning her taste in clothes and the
way she had done up the apartment. But he included a
judicious admixture of self-praise couched so as to escape
any stigma of boastfulness. He invented a brand-new
tale about the hunt for a man-eating tiger, to kill which
he had risked his life by acting as the decoy disguised in
the skin of a goat. It was so neatly framed that he
wished he had reserved his recently bought tiger skin
to go with this yarn rather than the one he had already
told her. In fact he was so pleased with his powers of
invention he almost failed to notice the effect the recital
was having on Mrs. Arnheim.

He broke off abruptly. She was looking distressed.

"I'm dreadfully sorry!" he exclaimed. "Does my story
upset you?"

She gave a cautious nod.

"Then I'll change the subject, my dear lady. I'm talking
too much about myself anyway. We ought really to be
discussing you, oughtn't we? That would be far more
interesting. Tell me . . ."

And smoothly on, averting disaster.

When he fetched their second drinks, he sat down
again much closer on the sofa. She edged away fractionally, but he kept talking—pouring oil on the troubled
woman, as he usually termed it to himself—and within a
short time she was accepting a light caress on the arm, a
squeeze of the hand, a meaningful smile, and some exaggerated physical compliments which evoked a kind of
wriggling response he hadn't expected to achieve before
at least a month's acquaintanceship. In his experience,
words far surpassed actions in the case of a woman like
her; typically, she would have driven her husband into
the arms of a mistress who was less revolted by all that
nasty "marital duty."

He tossed a mental coin, made up his mind, and leaned forward to kiss her.

And Mrs. Arnheim howled.

The consequences were swift and kaleidoscopic. For an instant he was petrified—he had never heard a cry like that from any human throat. Then there was a noise behind him, and he swung around on the sofa, thinking perhaps the maid had been awakened and come to see what the trouble was.

But the source of the sound was right here in the room—indeed, within arm's reach of him. From a hiding-place behind the sofa a man in black was rising to his feet. Two men. Three men. And the faces of all three were identical blanks.

His head spun. Jumping up, he stared from one to another of the impossible triplets. Mrs. Arnheim, who had jerked into an uncomfortable-looking position when she howled, moved not a muscle. She might have been a corpse.

Then the face of the man in the middle of the trio changed in the fashion he had seen last night, but not so quickly. Now he could follow every ghastly step of the leisurely process. The very bones beneath the flesh seemed to writhe and soften, and deformed into the semblance of the man who had denied trailing him.

The thread of Royston's self-control snapped. He launched himself at the man with the plastic face. Backed by his whole hard-muscled body, his fist slammed home on the point of the chin.

And bounced.

That wasn't a human jawbone he had hit. It felt more like tyre rubber.

He swayed on his feet, the truth forming hideously in his mind. The three men in black, no longer identical, returned his stare stonily.

"Aggressive, isn't he?" said the one in the middle. "I thought I might provoke a reaction by doing that, and I was right . . . Why did you call for help, Jeef?" It sounded like "Jeef."

"I lost my head, Kronze," said Mrs. Arnheim, stirring at last. "I thought he was going to bite me."

This is nightmare! Royston made a wild charge towards the door, determined to escape from this company of lunatics.

Without seeming to hurry Kronze was there ahead of him. Royston's fists swung and battered, but they left no mark on the mutable flesh, and arms as strong as hawsers pinioned him. His vision began to blur and whimpers escaped his slack lips.

"Do you agree that this is an exceptionally good specimen, Gruk?" said Kronze, disregarding the flailing blows Royston continued to rain on him. The other two conferred for a moment in low tones. Then Gruk spoke up.

"Yes, he looks very suitable. But hadn't you better quiet him? The racket he's making is likely to attract attention. Try not to damage the skin more than you can help."

The familiar phrase lanced through the mists in Royston's mind. *Try not to damage the skin!* Why, that must mean—

He felt himself lifted effortlessly from the floor, all his kicking and cursing in vain, and turned around. He wished wholeheartedly that he had not been turned, for now he could see that Mrs. Arnheim . . .

Or rather: the stalking-horse which he had called Mrs. Arnheim had rolled on its face on the floor and split up the middle. The hunter now emerging from the decoy was definitely not human. It was—it was . . .

Royston screamed. After a moment he had to stop in

order to be sick. Through the ringing in his ears he heard Kronze speak with professional enthusiasm.

"Wily beast, this! Did you hear the story he was telling Jeef about disguising himself as a goat to trap a tiger? I really thought for one moment he was on to us!"

"So did I," Jeef admitted, pushing aside the slack form of Mrs. Arnheim.

"You want me to preserve him right away?" Kronze inquired.

"Yes," instructed the one called Gruk. "We won't want to be bothered about feeding him on the voyage home."

Royston tried vainly to drown out the terrible words with another scream. He kept on, and on, until he felt Kronze's efficient imitation hands begin the business of turning him from a man into a museum piece.

The last thing he heard was the musing voice of the hunter saying something about the biggest game of all.

THE TROUBLE I SEE

When Joe Munday was four years old he ran screaming from behind a truck. The truck was a large and heavy one. It was parked in the steeply sloping street which was Joe's playground and the front yard of his home. Moments later the driver let his brake off, and his clutch failed. The truck rolled twenty feet backward before he could jam the brake on again and clamber white-faced to the ground to see if the kid he'd noticed on the sidewalk was okay.

When Joe Munday was seven, he was staying with his mother's sister on a farm thirty miles upstate. During a storm she was undressing him for his weekly bath. He tore loose from her and fled naked into pouring rain. As his aunt shouted imprecations after him from the doorstep, lightning struck the house and blinded her.

When Joe Munday was thirteen he refused to accompany the rest of the gang he hung around with when the leader wanted them to explore a deserted warehouse. The other kids met a man when they entered. Three months later the papers headlined a scandal: five boys sent to reformatory for peddling heroin to their school-friends.

When Joe Munday was fifteen he began to filch petty sums of money and make bets with them. He was never caught, because every bet he placed came up, until the local bookie refused to have anything to do with him. He had always managed to return the stolen cash and keep the profit.

"Good boy, that Joe Munday," people said. "Never gets in trouble!"

And he didn't, though it was taken for granted in the district where he lived that any kid would "be in trouble" sooner or later. So when he was seventeen he was beginning to suspect that he had something a little—extra.

Perhaps the "something extra" matured about then; at any rate the things which happened started to multiply to the point at which even someone with less than Joe's ration of astuteness would have had to scratch his head and wonder. Joe, being bright enough to figure the odds on such matters as getting caught before he'd returned the money he had "borrowed," had sufficient intelligence to understand that—somehow—he could sense when trouble was coming, and avoid it.

At first, his premonitions had only concerned danger. To his life, essentially. Lately they had grown more subtle, as though he had learned that there were other types of unpleasantness in addition to actual injury.

It was hard to believe in such a talent, even for him, and he was on the inside. So one time he ignored what it told him, and the result frightened him. That was the last time in his life Joe Munday wanted to be afraid. The sensation made him sick.

And so, at the age of seventeen years and nine months, Joe looked at his reflection in the mirror, and grinned. He had dark hair, and he dressed sharp, and aside from the pimples which he kept trying different brands of skin cream for he wasn't bad-looking. Good looks, and the knowledge that he need never be afraid again, sounded like a fair amount of capital for a man starting out in the world.

But exactly how do you set about investing capital which people don't know you've got, and which they wouldn't believe in if they were told about it? That problem puzzled Joe. The good looks aspect had already paid off; there was a girl on the next street who could certify to that. But the other . . .

He decided to go out and think it over.

He was on his way to the soda fountain at the nearest drugstore when he changed his mind and went into the bar on the corner instead. He had been there before, accompanied by a former acquaintance two years older than himself who had moved out of state and come back to brag to his old friends about his advancement in the world. Joe Munday had managed to tag along that time. This time, he told himself, he was going alone—and that was the way it would be from now on.

The bartender knew him, of course. Everyone in the neighbourhood knew everyone else, pretty well. And he wasn't apt to make trouble about Joe drinking under age. Well, what was a couple of months here or there, anyhow? So he let Joe have a beer without comment.

Joe didn't like beer very much, and in fact would have preferred a chocolate malted, but milk-shakes belonged to yesterday. With self-confidence that was not in the least feigned, he sat on the end stool before the bar and sipped slowly.

There weren't many other people in here. It was around two-fifteen and the lunch-hour crowd had dispersed. So after a quick look around the bartender opened the till and began to cash up. There seemed to Joe to be a great deal of money in the drawer.

When he had finished counting, the bartender put some change back to keep as a float, and called the

proprietor from in back. The boss sniffed unenthusiasti-
cally at the pile of paper and bags of coin.

"Stash it with yesterday's," he directed grumpily. "I'll
bank 'em both tomorrow. Not worth driving around to
the bank with that much."

The bartender nodded. Nobody was watching but Joe,
and Joe was sipping his beer. He packed the cash into
a canvas bag with a bank's name on it and took it in
back. A customer yelled for him as he went through the
door, so he hurried, didn't bother to close the door, gave
Joe a clear view of the cashbox he was stowing the money
in and that box's location relative to the window of the
room.

Joe turned a newborn idea over in his mind. With
relish. He submitted it for the approval of his talent,
and the talent agreed wholeheartedly.

They never did find out who stole that cashbox. Nobody dreamed of Joe Munday in connection with the
theft, of course—"Good boy, that Joe. Never in trouble
in his life. Not like some I could name."

It had always made Joe's mother proud to hear people
say things of that sort about her boy. As to his father
. . . Well, by now his father probably wouldn't recognize
him. It had been fourteen years since they saw each
other.

Too bad that she was going to be faced with heartbreak
now a second time. But the envy of the neighbours would
have been a petty reward for the risk involved if he'd
let anyone hear of his intention to quit the district and
improve himself. Likewise if he'd spent any of the money
he'd taken close to home. It burned his pocket in imagination, but he resolutely refrained from touching it for a
week, nine days, eleven days . . .

That should do it. A good unlikely number. He caught
a bus, moved to the state capital.

There he could spend money without anyone wondering where he'd got it.

Step one called for a visit to a clothing store. He consulted his talent when a very sharp outfit indeed caught his eye in the window. The talent said no; he realised why when he looked around and noted the ways in which the city differed from what he was accustomed to. Stifling his preferences remorselessly he invited the clerks in the store to show him a conservative suit that bespoke good taste. The effect pleased him; so did the service he was accorded. Clearly the clerks noticed the self-confidence in his eyes and realised subconsciously that here was someone to be reckoned with.

Step two involved finding somewhere to live. He rented a room on a street of handsome well-maintained houses that once had belonged to very wealthy families. He calculated dismally how rapidly its cost would diminish his funds; however, his talent insisted that he must have a good address. Not pretentious. Sound.

Step three was to go smelling for money.

It wasn't difficult. He'd got the feel of it now. Big cars were not so good a guide as small foreign ones, and that made him understand why his talent had turned down the sharply tailored clothes. Once you climbed to the level he was intending to reach, you became disillusioned with ostentation. Joe didn't happen to know the word ostentation, but he had an excellent conception of what it meant.

He employed his talent to decide where he should look for his first real boost upward in the world. He took his time. He discarded several attractive possibilities with regret, and settled on a man named Sarmer. There were good reasons for the choice. One was that Sarmer was rich—but so was everyone else Joe had considered, some more so than he. Two was that Sarmer didn't own a foreign car, though he could have afforded the most exclusive model made. He was strong on states' rights, prejudiced against foreigners and correspondingly biased in favour of local boys making good. Three was that although he had a daughter—an uncommonly beautiful girl, moreover—he had no son, though he desperately wanted one. His wife had died giving birth to a deformed boy, that also died. And now he would never sire the son he craved; his doctors had warned him he hadn't long to live.

Perfect.

He made himself as much a part of Sarmer's neighbourhood as he could. Conservative in everything, the old man had resisted the trend to the suburbs, and still lived in a house in the city not far from where Joe was lodging. It was easy to catch his eye now and then—coming on quiet, sober, always well-dressed—and to graduate to an occasional greeting: "Good morning, Mr. Sarmer! Miss Sarmer!" But not pushing things. Letting them move at their own speed.

It wasn't long before the greeting was returned, and Sarmer looked him over, seeming to wonder where he'd met this young man with the self-assured air. It wasn't long before Julie Sarmer was waving as she spotted him from her blue convertible, if one of her regular boyfriends wasn't with her.

And eventually there was a real conversation, and Sarmer liked him. Joe consulted his talent every time he uttered a word and the impression he made was favourable from all angles. He was in. Where he had always wanted to be without realising it. And one of these days —not long from now—Sarmer would say:

"Joe, you're a pretty good boy." (Modest interjected utterance of thanks.) "No, I mean it. Say, I've been thinking things over. Y'know, I'm not long for this world." (Shocked denial of such a possibility.) "Dammit, you

know it as well as I do. And as you also know, the son I
ought to have had . . ."

Only between now and that day there was a period of
waiting. Containing oneself in patience. Making ends
meet by devious means. Certain things made it especially
hard. There was Julie above all, slim, blond, exquisite
and expensive, and it cost him a deal of pillow-punching
and tossing at night to refrain from making overtures to
her as if she had been the girl on the next street back
home. But his talent warned him that to do so would
bring him to disaster. Julie looked down on him. She was
prepared to accept him as a protégé of her father's; she
didn't guess he was going to be her father's heir. So he
maintained a cool distance, though he could sense that
she was curious about him.

It was probably she who suggested that he be invited
to her nineteenth birthday party.

But instead of cultivating her, he cultivated her father
and the few old friends he'd invited to keep him company
while the house, as he put it, rang with that racket these
crazy kids go in for nowadays, and in response to ques-
tioning let it be known that he was orphaned, determined to make his own way in the world, not yet certain
of the best path for him to follow . . . It went down
Sarmer like milk down a baby.

Joe moved in.

He didn't go back home, not even to see his mother,
not even to see that girl on the next block. It would have
been inadvisable. He learned—deviously—that she was
pregnant, and realised exactly how many obstacles that
would have created in his way. He breathed a silent
prayer of thanks and forgot about her.

He was coming to recognise now that his talent worked
on two levels. One indicated impending disaster through
actions not his own, like that lightning strike when he
was seven. (He had been told about the episode of the

truck, but he didn't recall it.) The other indicated that
he was letting himself in for trouble of his own making.
In either case, of course, he had to figure a way out of the
trouble for himself. But it wasn't difficult.

For instance, out driving. Sarmer loaned him a car
without even being asked; he owned five. Wanting to
tear down a beautifully cambered high-speed curve, Joe
would listen to his talent and surprise any passenger he
might have by slowing to a decorous thirty. And then
around the bend there would be a truck-and-trailer jack-
knifed across his lane. That sort of thing gained him a
reputation as a brilliant driver.

His acquaintances were drawn from a different sphere
now. He was regarded as a bit of a curio, but since he
bore old man Sarmer's stamp of approval he was accepted. Sometimes. His driving ability earned him the
envy of a young sports-car fan who proudly invited him
to take the wheel of his new Lamborghini. Joe refused.
He didn't give an explanation, just refused. Angrily the
young man insulted him and jumped in and drove away.
He went three miles and was running at over seventy
when a front tyre blew out and he smashed through a
wall and killed himself.

Nobody knew about that incident, except Joe. And
the driver. But he was dead.

It did cross Joe's mind that maybe his refusal had made
the dead man so angry that he couldn't control the car
after the blow-out. But he hadn't actually known the
tyre would fail. He had only sensed that trouble lay that
way and he could avoid it by not getting into the car.

Joe changed during the next three years. He found it
more difficult than he had expected. There was a hell of
a lot to learn which he had never dreamed about. His
official reason for living in the Sarmer house was to act
as a kind of salaried companion to the old man. His

intention was to learn. Even so . . . He had had a misty
notion that making money the way Sarmer did was akin
to betting, and that he could simply apply his talents to
speculation in the stock market instead of gambling. But
just as the only way he could make bets come up was by
using stolen money which he had to return or else he'd
land in reform school, so he found that speculation employing Sarmer's money didn't activate his talent. If he
made an error, Sarmer would write it off to experience
and tell him to try again. He got around that one by
organising himself a bank loan he had no chance of re-
paying unless his guesses came off. That way he risked
losing both the money and Sarmer's confidence, a double
disaster.

Three years. He'd never really bothered with newspapers before, except maybe the sports section. Now he had
to study markets, and then he had to learn how the
foreign situation might affect prices, so he had to find out
how to use hints in the news-columns, rumours and
sheer guesswork to influence his selections. He did learn,
for his talent prevented him from making errors. The
situation could have struck people as fantastic: a boy
scarcely out of his teens enjoying Sarmer's complete trust,
already his right-hand man and with every chance of
being his successor; but naturally Joe did nothing which
would have made them decide it *was* fantastic. On the
contrary, when they thought the matter over in detail,
they had to admit that Sarmer had made a very logical
choice.

And so the long-expected day came when Sarmer
handed Joe a drink and told him to sit down and
hemmed and hawed and finally said that he thought Joe
was a pretty good boy. Excitement almost got the better
of Joe at that point. Not quite. If it had he would have
been scared of unforeseeable consequences, and he was
determined never to feel frightened again.

Sarmer hadn't intended to have this conversation quite yet, but his doctors had given him an ultimatum and his action had been precipitated. Joe was in.

Anyone else probably would have felt scared at the prospects which now opened up. Not Joe.

Someone who did was Julie Sarmer, and she said as much, but her father firmly forebade her to question his decision, and she wasn't really very interested in business matters, and pretty soon there wasn't much she could do about it because Sarmer died.

The evening after the funeral Joe consulted his talent and saw no trouble looming ahead, so he pointed out—quite tactfully—to Julie that whereas she was now merely a minor heiress with sharply limited income from a trust-fund (it was a sore point with Joe that the defining point had not been set lower, but after all she was Sarmer's flesh and blood), he was a young man going places, and if she wanted to come with him it would have to be on terms which he spelled out. He hadn't had any terms like that since the girl on the next street from home—his talent kept warning him of trouble when he felt inclinations towards girls in his new social circle—and the strain was getting hard to bear.

She slapped his face and walked out.

He took it comparatively philosophically, and discovered without much trying that he could make good the loss. That satisfied him for some months.

Everything else seemed to be lovely. He was now in a position to employ his talent to the fullest, for if he put a foot wrong he was really getting himself and no one else into trouble. Consequently he touched things and they turned, if not to gold, then to securities and bonds and extended holdings. A very satisfactory state of affairs.

A state of acute international tension was stimulating

the markets. New government contracts were being placed; the businesses which benefitted saw their shares climb like rockets. Joe was on to these rises as often as not. He had an extra incentive to exploit his talent, too; Julie had quarrelled with him and taken legal steps to question his right to administer her father's legacy, and unless he handled the estate competently he stood to have it taken away from him. But he was absolutely confident he had no cause to worry.

Until the morning he woke up feeling sick.

It wasn't physical sickness. It was something he hadn't experienced for so long he was hard put to it to recognise the sensation.

He was afraid.

At first he denied the fact. Then he resigned himself and grimly began to fight against it. But he found he was growing steadily more desperate as the day progressed—for he could not identify the source of the fear.

It rose in intensity, too, from moment to moment, presumably in direct ratio to the approach of the event he was afraid of. Twenty-four hours after it set in, it was already so bad that he couldn't employ his talent any more. He made a disastrous wrong guess and lost twenty thousand on a single deal. But the minor trouble caused by that was lost in the overwhelming certainty of far greater trouble from elsewhere.

Rivals who had been waiting and waiting for this to happen chuckled jubilantly and told one another, "I knew Joe Munday couldn't last!" Julie's lawyer heard, and called her up to hear the news. Joe guessed this must be happening, and found he was past caring.

All that he could establish about the catastrophe was that the danger was to come from above. Distractedly he stared at newspapers, watched TV, seeing news that a few days ago would have delighted him: mobilisation, new arms contracts, a great boost in federal spending.

From above! He thought wildly of missiles tipped with H-bombs. Thought of hiding in the bowels of the earth only to be buried alive beneath a ruined city. Thought of taking a plane to a lonely island, only to fall sick as invisible radioactive dust sifted down on him, and die in slow agony. Waves of fear eroded his mind like a sandcastle as the tide comes in.

Warning! He would have to give people a warning! But who first? Julie, perhaps—he rushed to the phone. She was with her lawyer. He called her there and gasped terrified words into the mouthpiece. She didn't seem to understand, but he had no time to explain further. He had to run. He had to do *something!*

Like an animal fleeing before a forest fire, Joe Munday ran from the room, down steps, into the street, staring this way and that in search of a cab. At that moment a man cleaning windows high overhead let go of the handle of his bucket, which fell. Fifty feet it managed to travel before it struck Joe Munday on the head and laid his brain bare to the incurious sky.

"War?" said the lawyer at that exact moment. "Man must be crazy!"

Among the first people to reach the spot where Joe lay was a newsboy. He kept control of his nausea long enough to put a poster over the ruined head. The lettering on it said, "War Risk Abates. Governments Back Down."

AN ELIXIR FOR THE EMPEROR

The roar of the crowd was very good to his ears, just as
the warm Italian sunshine was good on his body after
three years of durance in the chill of Eastern Gaul. Few
things made the general Publius Cinnus Metellus smile,
but now, for moments only, his hard face relaxed as he
made his way to the seat of honour overlooking the
circus. There was winding of buccae by trumpeters of
his own legions, but the sound was almost lost in the
shout of welcome.

This was what the populace liked from their generals:
a profitable campaign, a splendid triumph and a good
day of games to finish with.

Slowly the cries faded into the ordinary hum of conversation as Metellus took his place and glanced around
at his companions, acknowledging them with curt nods.

"It'll be good to see some decent games again, Marcus,"
he grunted to the plump elderly man next to him. "If
you'd had to sit through the third-rate makeshifts one
suffers in Gaul . . . You did as I asked you, by the
way?"

"Of course," lisped Marcus Placidus. "Though why you
were worried, I don't know. You brought enough live-
stock back with you to keep the arena awash for a week
—some of those Germanic wolves, in particular . . . No,

you're paying well. You'll get the best games Rome has seen in years."

"I hope so. I certainly hope so." Metellus let his eyes rove across the gaudy crowd. "But I'm not going to risk being cheated by some rascally lanista who wants to copper his bets! And . . . And things have changed here since I've been away. I feel out of touch."

He made the confession in a voice so low it reached no one but Marcus Placidus, and immediately looked as though he regretted uttering it at all. Marcus pursed his fleshy lips.

"Yes, there have been changes," he concurred.

After a brief pause, Metellus shifted on his chair. He said, "Well, now I'm here, where's the ringmaster? He ought to be on hand to open the show."

"We're waiting for the Emperor, of course," Marcus said with real or feigned surprise. "It would be an insult to begin without him."

"I didn't think he was coming!" Metellus exclaimed. His gaze fastened on the gorgeous purple-hung imperial box. "I thought the insult was going to pass in the opposite direction. After all, he's snubbed me before, hasn't he? You were there, Marcus! He said I bled my provinces white! A fine emperor, that wants no tribute for Rome! He doesn't even seem to realise that you have to keep your foot on the neck of those barbarians. If you don't, you wake up one morning with your throat slit. I've seen."

He started forward on his chair, staring about him for the missing ringmaster. "Nothing would please me better than to show the world what I think of his milk-and-water notions. I'm the editor of these games, and I say when they open!"

Marcus laid a restraining hand on the general's arm. He said apologetically, "The people wouldn't stand for it, you know."

"I know nothing of the sort! Since when would a Roman crowd prefer to sit broiling in the sun like chickens on a spit, rather than start the games?"

"Since you've been away, perhaps," Marcus murmured, and hauled his bulky body out of his chair. "Here he is now, anyway."

Scowling, Metellus also stood up. Shields clanged as the ranks of the guard completed the perfectly drilled movements of the salute, and the yell went up from the crowd. *The* yell—not just from the bottom of the lungs, but from the bottom of the heart. It went on. It lasted longer than the applause which had greeted Metellus, and seemed still to be gaining volume when the Emperor took his place.

As the roar echoed and re-echoed, the general clenched his fists. When, two years before, a courier had brought the news of Cinatus' accession, together with the warrant for the renewal of his proconsulship, Metellus had shrugged his shoulders. It was a wonder, of course, that they had ever allowed the old man to assume the imperial toga in succession to his childless nephew —whose short and bloody reign was memorable to Metellus for one thing: his chance to pick the plum of Eastern Gaul.

But with rival factions sprouting all over the Empire, it was probable the old man had been chosen because he wouldn't offend too many influential people. He certainly had not been expected to last so long. Or to handle his impossible task so well . . .

"Aren't they ever going to stop screaming?" Metellus snarled. "Who's editing these games, anyway?"

"You don't understand how they feel," was Marcus' only reply.

At that moment Cinatus, having made himself comfortable, caught Metellus' eye and shook his head in the Greek affirmative that was one of his few affectations. As though by magic the giant ringmaster popped into view in the arena.

"*At* last," grunted Metellus, and signalled for the games to be opened.

After the ritual procession, the ringmaster took his stand before the imperial box. All talking died away as the crowd waited eagerly to learn which of the many fabulous acts they'd just had a foretaste of would constitute the first spectacle.

"What did you decide to start with?" Marcus inquired behind his hand. "You were in two minds when I spoke to you yesterday."

"A perfect item, I think," Metellus answered. "It should put the crowd in a good humour straight away."

"A battle!" screamed the ringmaster. "Of the sun-baked South—against the frigid North! Six wild Germanic wolves from the forests of Eastern Gaul, brought hither by special command of the general—"

The next words were lost in a shout of excitement. Marcus gave a nod. "Ah, the wolves!" he commented. "I said they looked promising. But against what? Each other?"

"Not quite," Metellus said. "You'll see."

Once more the ringmaster bellowed. "And opposing them . . . !" He turned with a flourish, and all eyes followed the movement as a gate was thrown back to admit into the arena—head bowed to avoid a final blow from his jailer—an elderly dark-skinned man clad only in a ragged kilt and worn sandals after the Egyptian pattern, whose back was laced with the marks of the scourge. In one hand he clasped a sword, which he seemed not to know what to do with.

A gale of laughter went up from the crowd, in which Metellus joined rather rustily. "Excellent," he muttered to Marcus. "I told my procurator to find someone—some criminal—who would look really ridiculous. And there he is. Afterwards, you see, there's a giant bull—"

"I warn you," said Marcus in a very flat voice, "the Emperor is not laughing."

The general swung around. Indeed, Cinatus' face was set in a stern frown. He whispered to one of his attendants, who called to the ringmaster over the front of the box.

"Caesar desires to know with what crime this old man is charged!"

At a gesture, the ringmaster's assistants caught hold of the dark man and dragged him across the sand to answer for himself. He seemed to have recovered his wits, for as he straightened and looked up he gave a passable salute with his sword.

"My name is Apodorius of Nubia, O Caesar! And the crime of which I am accused is one I freely confess. I hold that neither you nor any other man who has assumed the purple thereupon became a god."

A low o-o-oh! went around the circus. Metellus sat back, satisfied. Surely Cinatus would not take that lightly.

But a hint of a smile played on the Emperor's lips. He spoke again to his aide, who relayed the question: "Why say you so?"

"Gods are not made by the will of men, and not all the words in the world can create divinity!"

"By the same token, then," came the good-humoured answer, "not all the talk in the world can unmake a god. Ringmaster, release this man, for it pleases Caesar to be merciful."

Aghast, Metellus turned to Marcus. "Can I believe my ears? Does he intend to ruin my games, as well as insulting me about the way I ran my province? Surely the people will not stand for this!"

"They are standing for it," said Marcus calmly. "Can you hear any objections?"

Indeed there were very few, quickly drowned out by a roar of cheers.

"But how is this possible?" Metellus demanded.

"You don't understand," said Marcus again. "They love their Emperor."

Though the rest of the show proceeded without interruption, Metellus hardly paid any attention. He sat with a scowl carved deep on his features, disturbed only when he growled—at frequent intervals—that it was a plot to make his accomplishments look small, that Cinatus was jealous of his popularity with the plebs. Marcus endured his complaints patiently, but it was a relief when the last item on the programme ended and the sated crowd began to force their way towards the exits. Rising with a curt word of farewell, and an even curter salute to Cinatus, Metellus ordered his retinue to clear a way to the street and stormed from the circus.

Following more slowly, looking thoughtful, Marcus Placidus listened to the comments of the departing audience. As he passed one young couple—an elegant and handsome youth accompanied by a pretty girl whom he had noticed in a front-row seat on the shadow side, naked as was the custom among the more expensive courtesans—he eavesdropped with the skill of long practice.

"Good games," the youth said.

"Was it not gracious of Caesar to pardon that old man?" the girl countered.

"It was so. We have seen many wear the purple who would rather have ordered that the wolves' teeth be specially sharpened because the meat on his old bones must be tough!"

"Would that such an emperor could be with us for ever!"

Marcus stopped dead in his tracks for the space of a

heartbeat, and then continued forward. After a while he did something quite out of keeping with his senatorial dignity: he began to hum a popular song which was going the rounds of the Roman brothels.

He was humming it again when his litter was set down before the house of Metellus late that evening, but under the astonished gaze of his torch-bearer—who doubtless knew where the song was current—he composed himself and followed the path to the door.

Over the plashing of the little fountain in the atrium he heard an enraged yell in Metellus' parade-ground voice. "If that's someone to see me, tell him to come along with the rest of the *clientes* in the morning!"

"It is the senator Marcus Placidus, General," said the respectful nomenclator, and Metellus gave a grunt which the slave interpreted as permission to show the caller in.

The general was reclining on a couch with a jug of Falernian wine at his side. A pretty Greek slave was massaging his neck.

"It had better be important, Marcus," he said shortly. "I'm not in the best of tempers, you know. And you know why!"

"It is."

"All right. Make yourself comfortable. Pour the senator some of this filthy Falernian!" he added to the Greek girl, and she hastened to obey.

Marcus spilt a drop in ritual libation and swigged a healthy draught of the wine. Then he set the cup aside and produced something from the folds of his toga. On the open palm of his plump pink hand he showed it to Metellus. It was a rose.

The general came to an abrupt decision. "Get out," he told his slaves, and as they vanished soundlessly he added, "Well?"

"How would you like to be Emperor, Metellus?"

"I know you too well, or I should think you'd been

chewing ivy, like a bacchante!" the general said causti-
cally. "Or have you changed along with everything else
in Rome?"

"I assure you I'm perfectly serious. You were probably
going to point out that Cinatus is firmly ensconced—
which is true. It's also true that the court, and all
Rome, are less turbulent than they've been in my lifetime. But Cinatus has made enemies apart from yourself.
You know about my grounds for disliking him, to begin
with."

"Something to do with a debt, wasn't it?" Metellus
said, and gave a harsh laugh.

"A trifling matter," Marcus told him. "A question of a
few tens of thousands. But it was the principle of the
thing. He gave judgment against me, and I had to resort
to most undignified methods to recover what I was owed.
If I hadn't needed it so badly—"

"You're being strangely candid."

"I wish you to see how I would benefit from a change
of Caesar. Others like me have been—shall we say,
embarrassed by decisions on the part of Cinatus? A petty
slight against someone in my position can rankle and
ultimately fester. I suspect that those others whose co-
operation I intend to enlist will agree chiefly because
they imagine that once *we* have tumbled this immovable
Caesar, it will be a matter of weeks before *they* topple
his successor and install their own favourite. But I think
they would find you hard to shift. Besides, you are popular with the plebs already. What more natural choice
than our most successful general to assume the purple?"

"And how do you propose bringing this minor miracle
to pass?"

Marcus told him.

At the end Metellus had a faraway look in his eyes.
"Suppose, though, that Cinatus finds out from whom the
suggestion originated? Will he not smell a rat?"

"Trust me for that, Metellus. I can arrange matters so

subtly that the actual proposition will come from someone he relies on implicitly—who will himself believe he's making the suggestion in good faith."

"Ye-es," said Metellus doubtfully. He rose and began to pace the floor, head down, hands clasped behind his back. "But will Cinatus act on the proposal when it's made? Won't his accursed scepticism cause him to laugh the idea to scorn? Oh, Marcus, it will never succeed!"

"You're a man used to direct action," the senator said. "You're ill accustomed to the twists and turns of a court intrigue. I, however"—he gave a modest cough—"have some not inconsiderable skill in the latter field. I've already thought of the risk you mention. I'll forestall it by having Cinatus consent in order to be rid of those who keep plaguing him with concern about his health."

"We'll consult the auspices," Metellus said suddenly. "If they're favourable, I'm with you."

Marcus smiled like a contented cat. He had not expected so swift a victory.

First, he planted a rumour that the Emperor was a sick man. Since Cinatus was elderly, not to say old, people were ready to believe it. So often did he hear the whispered report from others, he soon almost credited it himself. Every time he saw Cinatus he studied him for signs of infirmity. However, the Emperor remained annoyingly hale.

So he planted his second seed. This was a single nebulous concept, whose pattern of growth he had chosen with extreme care. And, as the idea was relayed to more and yet more courtiers, it took exactly the form he had hoped for.

When it came finally to the ears of Cinatus himself it did so—as Metellus had been promised—from a close friend who honestly believed he was making a valuable suggestion.

"If it were only possible for Caesar to remain with us for another twenty years, we might see Rome even greater than she has been in the past."

"Faugh!" said Cinatus. "I'm fifty-four years old, and if I last another five under the strain of your pestering I'll have done well. Besides, who told you I wanted to put up with twenty more years of this job?" And, to drive home his point, he finished, "Anyhow, there's no way of making an old man young, so the notion is ridiculous."

"Is it?" his friend persisted. "There are stories of men who have chanced on potions to confer long life and good health. In Asia they tell of a king who discovered such a drug—a herb—but a serpent stole it from him before he could use it. And the Jews claim that their ancestors lived to an age comparable with that of the heroes—seven hundred years!"

"I'm not a Jew, and I'm rather glad," said Cinatus feelingly, for at that time those intransigent inhabitants of Palestine were once more in spirited revolt against their Roman rulers. "Are you suggesting I should become one?" he added with a glare. "If so, you can precede me. I'm told the process is rather painful!"

"Not at all, not at all," soothed the trusted friend, and then and there recounted the wholly fictitious news Marcus had so dexterously invented.

Cinatus did not yield at once. But after a month's importuning by more and more of his oldest friends, he gave in—as predicted—for the sake of peace and quiet.

"What did I tell you?" Marcus said smugly when he next called on Metellus. "Listen, I have the text of the proclamation here—it's to be made public tomorrow."

"How did you get hold of it?" the general demanded, and Marcus raised a reproving eyebrow.

"Do I inquire the secrets of your strategy? I think I may keep my own methods under the rose, then! But hear this. After the usual trifles about the graciousness of Caesar and how everyone wants him to reign a thousand years, it goes on:

"'If any man bring to Rome medicine which after trial proves to bestow long life and good health he shall be richly rewarded, but if any man bring a medicine which is useless he shall be banished from the city and if any man bring a medicine which is harmful he shall be punished and if any man bring a poison his life shall be forfeit.'"

Apologetically re-folding the wax tablets he had been reading from, he added, "Three penalties for one hope of reward, as you notice. I'm sorry, but that was the only way we could get Cinatus to seal the proclamation."

"Hmm!" Metellus rubbed his chin. "Do men bet against such odds in this strange Cinatified Rome of ours? I mean, will there be any candidates at all?"

"Beyond a doubt. They may not love Cinatus as much as they say they do, but they'll come—to puff some cult or other, or for the hope of gain, or for notoriety . . . And anyway I've arranged a steady supply of quacks to keep the interest of the plebs whipped up."

Metellus gave a reluctant smile. "Yes, I've noticed the city is full of sorcerers and favour-seeking acolytes of the mystery cults. Some of them even have the gall to come howling at *my* door. Well, let's assume a man turns up and produces some noxious drench: what then?"

"Why, then we try their potions on some slaves, do we not? For instance, you're aware that Cinatus has a trusted body-slave, a Greek called Polyphemus for his one eye?"

"I've seen him," Metellus granted.

"In your name I've offered him his manumission if he helps us. He's made good use of his position at court, and has a small private fortune. But Cinatus won't release him—says he depends on him too much. It's the worst mistake he's committed.

"Now, this Polyphemus thinks he can outwit me. Of course I have no intention of letting him go free with such a secret, and he suspects this, but he wants his liberty so much he's willing to gamble on the chance of blackmailing me afterwards." Marcus sat back with a pleased expression.

"What secret are you talking about?"

"Why—! See: when *our* sorcerer, *our* doctor, comes to offer his potion to the Emperor, it will be something no more harmful than water."

"Not so harmless, that," grunted Metellus, thinking of the stinking stagnant liquid he had often encountered in the field. "But go on."

"Well, it's a detail we can settle. Make it a tasteless powder to be administered in wine, if you prefer." Marcus dismissed the point with an airy wave. "But I've arranged for Polyphemus, over the next few weeks, to feign occasional illness, severe enough to make Cinatus worry about losing him. When the medicine has been tested on some slaves and proved at worst innocuous, he's then going to volunteer to be the last experimental subject and will promptly make a miraculous recovery.

"It will then be the task of this same one-eyed Greek to give the potion to Cinatus. He'd trust no one else to administer it. And what he gives the Emperor will be —ah—stronger than water."

"I see. You're devious, Marcus, but clever, I concede! So we shall have to find culprits: the pretended doctor, and while we're about it, why not the one-eyed slave? Yes, neat and tidy like a good plan of battle!" In an access of uncharacteristic enthusiasm Metellus almost clapped his hands, but cancelled the impulse on realising it would bring slaves into the room. Then his mood changed.

"We'd better move swiftly, though! For if I mistake not,

people are beginning to forget the tribute my campaigns brought to Rome."

"We shall be swift enough," smiled Marcus, and stowed in the bosom of his toga the tablets on which was inscribed the proclamation even now being carried to the four corners of the world.

Long, long before the sages of Egypt and the Druid mystics of Europe heard the news and began their preparations, the word came to Apodorius the Nubian as he shivered over a wood fire in a stinking little inn beside the Tiber. He was awaiting a ship that would bear him back to Africa.

Already he had travelled very far. He had sat at the feet of philosophers in Athens retailing the wisdom of their ancestors like parrots; he had bowed in the temples of Alexandria and the sacred groves of Asia; he had been initiated into mystery cults from Persia to the Pillars of Hercules; he had acquired very much knowledge. In fact, as he disputed anew with priests and adepts in every place he visited, he had begun to suspect that few men anywhere had studied so widely and absorbed so much.

And the suspicion had given him a certain courage.

The fact that a whim of Caesar had saved him an agonised death in the arena counted little with him. He was not as attached to his mortal frame as he had been when he was a youth. He cared more that he had sensed in the elderly Cinatus a quality unique among the many rulers he had seen: hard-headed common sense.

Apodorius, though Romans had almost cost him his life, was not blind to the benefits Roman mastery had brought to the world. He had been in many countries enjoying more peace and greater prosperity than ever under governments of their own. But should Caesar be weak, his deputies corrupt, the Empire could—did— bring misery.

The world needed the Empire. The Empire needed a good Caesar. Apodorius made up his mind.

Publius Cinnus Metellus *Augustus*—Caesar himself, latest of the wearers of the imperial purple—yawned. If he had been able to find a way around the right of all citizens to appeal in person to the Emperor, he would have done so. He hated dealing with petty squabbles, disputes over money, pretended claims against judges he had himself appointed . . . Unfortunately it was unavoidable. People who had enough funds to bribe their way past the various subordinates with whom he had surrounded himself, however, were also rich enough to be influential, and he had to continue going through the motions at least where they were concerned.

Marcus Placidus felt differently, of course. He enjoyed watching people scheme and weave devious plans, for the eventual pleasure of outwitting them. Metellus prevented his face from lapsing into a frown—just in time—as the senator himself entered the audience hall.

Too clever by half, the Emperor thought. *Something might have to be done about him . . .*

"Well?" he demanded. "I understood today's audience was at an end."

"I think," Marcus murmured, "you may be interested in one more of those who have been waiting at the door. Look, O Caesar!"

The doors opened again. Through them stepped a dark-skinned figure, very thin, old, ragged, yet bearing himself with a certain dignity. To his chest he clutched something reddish-brown—a pottery jar sealed with a lump of wax. He bowed vaguely in Metellus' direction; it was obvious that his sight was failing and an usher had to push him towards the throne.

Metellus' first impulse was to demand who had let this flea-ridden bag of bones into the hall. Then he checked.

If Marcus had expressed interest in him, there must be a reason. He puzzled for a long moment, and at last said, "I see nothing significant about this scarecrow!"

"No? Think back, O Caesar," Marcus urged. "Think what that jar he clutches may contain. Do you not recall a day of games following your triumph when—?"

"That Nubian? The one Cinatus pardoned—may the empty-headed fool drown in Styx! Why, of course!" Metellus snapped his fingers. "Ap . . . something. Apodorius!"

The Nubian, apparently more by guesswork than sight, for it was plain to Metellus now that his eyes were filmed with cataracts, halted facing him.

"Caesar remembers me?" he said with faint astonishment.

"Indeed we do," Metellus confirmed grimly. Watching, Marcus allowed a sly smile to creep across his face.

As though vaguely troubled by the sound of the Emperor's voice, Apodorius hesitated, lovingly stroking the earthenware pot he cradled in his skinny arms. Seeming to draw confidence from it, he spoke up.

"I come in answer to a proclamation of Caesar more than a year ago, which said that if a man brought medicine to Rome for the health of Caesar he would be rewarded. I want no reward. You gave me my life, and in return"—he thrust his jar forward convulsively —"I bring you *everlasting* life!"

There was a long slow silence, which soughed through the hall like an ice-cold wind.

It was broken by an undignified gurgle of laughter from Marcus. Metellus shut him up with a murderous glare and leaned forward.

"Why have you delayed so long, Apodorius?" he asked silkily.

"I beg Caesar's indulgence! It was often hard to come by the ingredients, so I had to search far and wide."

"And why, seeing you have this medicine, are you yourself old and sick, and nearly blind?"

"The ingredients were costly," said the old man apologetically. "I had little money. I could buy no more than would make one dose . . ." He tapped the pot. "And that dose is for Caesar, not for me."

Metellus slapped the arm of his throne. "Know, O stupid conjurer, that your kind is not welcome in Rome!"

"But—but there are no others of my kind, Caesar. None but I could have brewed this elixir!"

"If your eyes were unveiled," Metellus said, rising to his feet so that he towered over the Nubian, "you would realise that I am not Cinatus, who spared your worthless life in the arena, but Metellus, who ordered you into it! And sorcerers of your breed are unwelcome because one like you came to Rome offering an elixir which proved to be poison and from whose effects Cinatus—Augustus—died."

At each of the last three words Apodorius winced, as if under successive blows. Slowly, slowly, he lowered his cherished jar. He stood very still, a broken man.

"Guards!" barked Metellus. Two brawny soldiers closed on the Nubian. "Take that jar from him."

A fist moved swiftly and seized it.

"Break the seal and pour this charlatan's muck down his own throat!"

The order galvanised the old man. He stiffened, and babbled the beginnings of a plea. A broad palm shut his mouth for him.

"We notice you are less eager to drink your elixir than to have Caesar drink it," Marcus said dryly. "Go ahead, soldier!"

Forcing Apodorius' mouth open, the man spilt rather than poured a clear greyish liquid from the jar between the Nubian's bare gums. A quick jab in the stomach made him swallow convulsively, and again, and until the jar was empty.

"Let him go," Metellus directed, and Apodorius slumped to the floor in a faint.

"As I thought," Marcus murmured. "Oh, the subtlety of these philosophers!"

Metellus ignored him. He was too pleased with his own acumen to listen to self-praise from the stout senator. "Now take that bundle of skin and bones and dump it in the Tiber," he instructed the guards. "And let me hear no more of sorcerers."

"*Just* as I thought," Marcus said more loudly, and Metellus rounded on him.

"And what do you mean by that?" he demanded.

"Reflect, O Caesar! Is it truly possible that a man abiding anywhere in the Empire should have failed to hear of your succession, or that having failed he should not have learned the facts on reaching Rome? No, doubtless this fellow thought that by pretending he was so blind he imagined he was offering his potion to Cinatus he could make you as gullible as his old benefactor and induce you to take his poison."

"Then why should he not have come sooner?" frowned Metellus.

The question troubled him for a few moments; moreover Marcus had no immediate answer. Then he dismissed it from his mind and called for wine, wishing he had conceived a more spectacular fate than mere drowning for this skilful would-be regicide.

Consciousness returned after what seemed like the passage of aeons to Apodorius. He was lying on a rough and hard support, a wooden bench, and was so astonished to find he had not been thrown in the river already that he sat up by pure reflex before he had taken in his surroundings. For the first time in many months he did not feel his usual twinge of rheumatism.

His eyes, too, were clearer. Though the light was bad, he could see he was in a stone-walled cell; its ceiling oozed green damp. A grille of metal bars cut him off from another, identical cell, where a man with one eye sat counting the fingers of his left hand.

Seeing the Nubian rise, however, he let the hand fall to his side and cautiously approached the bars. When he spoke, it was with a strong Greek accent.

"You're the last of the conjurers, aren't you? You're going to Father Tiber tonight, aren't you? Oh, yes! You've come back, and I knew you would, because I'm still here and I'm trapped the same as you."

He talked with a kind of explosive bitterness in which insanity rang dully like a counterfeit coin on a money-changer's table.

"Marcus Placidus did for us both very nicely," the one-eyed man went on. "I thought I was cleverer than he was, but I was wrong, and he proved it to me. He proved it slowly, for a long, lo-ong, LO-O-ONG TIME!"

From a conversational level his voice rose to a screech. As though challenging Apodorius to doubt his words he thrust the stump of his right arm through the grille. It had no fingers left. The thumb was a mere blob of flesh and the skin from palm to elbow was seared with the marks of the torturer's iron.

"Who are you?" Apodorius said slowly.

"Polyphemus," said the Greek, and giggled. "Only I'm luckier than the real Polyphemus. Marcus didn't put my eye out with a hot stick, oh no! Marcus isn't as clever as Odysseus, but I'm not as clever as Marcus."

Abruptly he altered his tone again, and now cocked his head so that his one-sided gaze could study his new companion's face. "You came too late to poison Caesar, you know," he said. "I did it a long time ago. Marcus told me he'd manumit me for it, but he lied—he was clever! He proved it," he added inconsequentially, and thrust his left arm also through the grille so that he could count its fingers again, this time by touching them in turn to the blob marking the site of his other thumb.

Apodorius felt facts mesh together in his mind. Hoping against hope for a few minutes' clarity from the Greek's disordered brain, he spoke as things presented themselves to him.

"It was a plot of Marcus Placidus' to poison Cinatus. You pretended to be a doctor and—no, that can't be right. You said you knew I'd be back . . . Ah. You were imprisoned here with the man who posed as a doctor and brought poison instead of medicine, who'd been put up to it by Marcus, and hence presumably by Metellus. You must have been one of Cinatus' slaves, promised your freedom if you substituted poison for the elixir."

"You know all that," Polyphemus said petulantly. "Why go on about it? You gave me the poison before you went to Caesar with water. Water! Even water can kill you, if you drink as much of it as there is in the Tiber!"

Footsteps sounded in an echoing corridor. Polyphemus moved away from the grille and listened intently. "I think they're coming to take you away," he said, unholy joy in his voice. "But you'll be back. Sooner or later you'll be back. You keep coming and going, but . . . I'm the proof, you know. The senator told me so. If ever he can't cope with Metellus, he said, he'll use me to prove it was a plot of Metellus' to poison Caesar. I hope he doesn't have to use me as proof, because they torture slaves before they make them talk, and I've been tortured. Did you know?"

He finished with a pathetic attempt at confidence, "But Marcus will be able to handle Metellus! Marcus is clever! Marcus is clever! Marcus is—"

"Shut your mouth, you!"

Apodorius turned, not too quickly, to see that the speaker was an officer of the guard who had halted beyond the grating set into the door of his cell. Bolts jarred

back as the soldiers accompanying him heaved on their
handles. The officer stepped inside.

"Awake, are you?" he grunted. "Hah! Can't have been
very powerful poison, then. Still, no matter—it will please
Caesar when I tell him you were conscious enough to
enjoy the taste of the river." He gestured to the soldiers,
and they moved purposefully forward. It would have
been senseless to offer resistance; Apodorius let them do
as they liked.

When his arms had been lashed behind his back and
his legs so hobbled he could barely stumble along, he was
jabbed into the corridor at the point of the officer's sword.
The sound of Polyphemus counting—up to five, and then
again up to five—died slowly in the distance.

"If it weren't ridiculous," the officer muttered, "I'd
swear you were actually the better for that muck you
swallowed. Not that it's going to make any difference
now."

He swung open a door and they emerged on a stone
ledge, under which the river ran chuckling. It was very
dark, and the night breeze had a chill to it.

"*Vale*, brewer of elixirs," the officer said, and drove the
point of his sword deep into Apodorius' left buttock. Yelling, he plunged into the water—and vanished.

The soldiers waited long enough to be sure he would
not surface, and dispersed with no further thought of the
matter. It was all in their day's work.

But deep in the swift-flowing Tiber Apodorius was
hoarding his breath, conscious mainly of how glad he
was they hadn't sewn him in a sack before they threw
him in.

"At this hour?" said Marcus Placidus irritably. "Who?"

"He is a Nubian, senator," the slave explained, unaware
of the effect he was about to have on Marcus' state of
mind. "He is very wet and muddy, and if he had not

sworn by all the gods that it was a matter of life and death I should have kicked him into the street. But he says I must tell you that his name is Apodorius."

"Wine," Marcus said faintly. "Help me to a couch. And quick—*get that man in here!*"

"I have come, Senator," said the unmistakable voice of Apodorius from the curtained doorway. Marcus' eyes bulbed in his fat face. He gasped and swayed, and the slave anxiously aided him to the nearest couch.

"I regret the state in which I call on you," the Nubian went on. "But Tiber is at the best of times an unclean river, and I had some trouble breaking free of my bonds."

"Come—come here," whispered Marcus. "Let me— No! You, slave! Touch this man and see if he is substantial!"

Astonished, the man obeyed. "He is warm flesh," he reported. "But slippery with mud, as you observe."

"No ghost . . . Praise be, praise be! What do you want with me?" Marcus wheezed.

"I have a grim kind of business with Caesar," Apodorius answered dryly. "But why should I approach him when it is known to all Rome and the Empire that the words are his and the thoughts are yours?"

Marcus could not help preening himself a little, and recovered some of his ordinary composure. "Slave!" he rapped. "Cleanse this man—he's my guest! Wipe him, give him a fair new toga, bring wine for him, and be quick!"

And he watched as his orders were put into effect, unashamedly goggling.

"I find it hard to accept that you're here," he said at last. "Still, I must do so or never again believe my senses. And such a trick as you must have employed to escape is one worth knowing. Speak!"

Refreshed, neatly clad, Apodorius gave a smile.

"Why, Senator, my elixir which you took for a lie was potent enough! Ask the guards who dropped me in the

Tiber whether they did not see me sink with arms and legs bound!"

"I . . ." Marcus hesitated. "Granting that's true, why have you come to me?"

"To offer a bargain. A fair one, I think. You are in a position to give me what I most desire: revenge upon Metellus for what he did to me. Likewise I am able to give you what you want—what I already have against my will. I doubt you'll care much which Caesar wears the purple when you wield the power."

Marcus leaned forward with greed brilliant in his eyes.

"Destroy Metellus," Apodorius said, "and I will give you my elixir."

Marcus pulled at his lower lip. After a moment's reflection he said cannily, "Your elixir! How do I know it's not a sham? How do I know you weren't pretending to be old and blind, and sloughed the appearance of age as easily as you slipped your bonds in the river?"

Apodorius winced and rubbed a chafed ankle. "Do not term that 'easy,' Senator," he complained. "But I have proof for you. Setting aside the point that no hale man with any alternative open would have gone willingly to be torn apart by wolves—you remember?—I have taken so great a dose of my medicine that I am growing younger almost by the hour. See!" He opened his mouth and indicated his visibly toothless gums. "I feel an ache which may even portend . . ."

Marcus rubbed his finger along the shrivelled flesh and gaped in awe. Surely no conjurer's deception could make sharp new teeth grow in an ancient's jaw!

Even so, it was not until three days later when the first tooth was cut, gleaming and indisputable, that he sealed the bargain Apodorius had proposed. Then he was committed. In truth, what was it to him if Metellus went down to join the shades? An immortal man could become the power behind not one Caesar, but all Caesars!

Apodorius watched him grow drunk on the heady liquor of his dream.

He asked for what he wanted, and Marcus supplied it with no demur at the cost, which—as had already been said—was immense. The senator's desire for secrecy suited him; in a quiet room at the back of the house he worked with the strange mixture of substances bought for him, and weeks slipped by.

After two months, however, Marcus was at the limit of his patience, and Apodorius judged it unwise to make him wait any longer.

Accordingly he waited on him when he returned from the Senate, and to his fevered demand for news of progress gave a simple headshake of affirmation.

"Yes, I have prepared the elixir again. It goes quicker when one can buy from a bottomless purse instead of having to beg and even steal . . . What have you done to keep your side of the bargain?"

Marcus rolled his eyes to heaven and clasped his hands. He whispered, "I have arranged that next time Caesar goes to the circus a pillar below his box will be loosened. An elephant will be goaded into terror and caused to break the pillar down. If Metellus is not trampled to death, the care of such doctors as I have recommended to him can be counted on to help him join the shades."

"Good," said Apodorius. "Then come with me."

Marcus entered the room where the Nubian had been working, and stopped dead. Everything had been taken from it—all the pans, jars, braziers—all but a single small table on which rested a crock containing a greyish fluid. His eyes lit up as he recognised the colour of the liquid that had been forced down Apodorius' throat.

He stretched out his hand towards it, and then checked himself. "No!" he croaked. "You first! Sip it before I do—and do no more than sip it, mind!"

"Have no fear," said Apodorius quietly. "I have made enough this time for more than a single dose." He picked up the crock and set it to his lips.

Marcus' eyes, alert for any hint of deception, followed his movements as he drank three slow mouthfuls of the stuff. Then he replaced the crock and rested his hand on the table to steady himself.

"You may feel a little giddy at first," he husked. "Remember, when I was forced to drink before Caesar I fell in a swoon. But you are not so old and weak as I was then."

His breathing grew easier and he straightened. Convinced there was no trickery, and impatient beyond endurance, the senator seized the crock and drained it in frantic gulps.

When he set it down, it was with a crash that shattered it and sent the shards flying across the floor. A burning began in his stomach. Dark veils crept across his vision as he sought to fix his eyes on the Nubian's face.

Through a rushing torrent of pain he heard Apodorius' voice, very cool, very detached.

"You are a dead man, Senator."

"What?" he whimpered. "What?"

"I have drunk the elixir—the real elixir. You have not. In that crock was the strongest poison I have ever found. I drank it, and I live. But you die."

Marcus Placidus clutched his belly as though he would squeeze the poison from it like water from a sponge. But blueness was already showing on his lips and around his fingernails. In a moment he could stand no longer, and crumpled to the floor. His eyes rolled; his chest barrelled out in a final despairing gasp of air. And he was dead.

"But that will make no difference to Metellus," Apodorius said to the corpse. "Not yet. Even if his doctors save him after the accident at the circus. I am sure, Senator, you were sufficiently skilled in flattery to let

him imagine your decisions were his own. By himself—
well, he is no Cinatus!"

And, his thoughts ran on, *his fall will probably bring
the Empire down* . . . Another wave of murdered Caesars, and then barbarian invasions from the outskirts of
the Empire—oh, the ultimate collapse of so mighty an
edifice would take centuries, but it was now inevitable.

And afterwards?

"We shall see," murmured Apodorius. And then cor-
rected himself with wry amusement. "Or rather: I shall
see!"

He dipped his finger in a drop of poison which remained in a fragment of the broken crock, and thought of
the care he had taken to make its colour exactly the same
as that of the real elixir. He still felt queasy from the
three mouthfuls he had swallowed. Enough of that poison
would perhaps pierce his invulnerability.

Rising, he spoke to the air.

"Does it make you smile, Cinatus Augustus, there in
the land of shades? You gave me my life, and I've avenged
you. But Metellus outdid your gift! He gave me everlasting life, and because of that I have destroyed him.
Do you understand, Cinatus? I think you do. I think if I
had come to you, you would have turned me away.

"Perhaps, then, I would have been offended. But now I
know why I brewed my elixir for an emperor, and not for
me."

He stared down at the poison in the broken crock, and
did not see it. He was contemplating the endless centuries ahead, and feeling himself grow cold.

"Next time I brew," he said, "which will I choose?
This? Or a renewal of the other?"

The fat dead body of the senator did not answer him.
Its mouth, though, was already curved in the sardonic
corpse's leer known as the Hippocratic smile.

The doorbell sounded.

Hal Page had been attending to two final tasks: first, checking around the apartment and making sure everything was ready for this, which was going to be one *hell* of a party; second, trying to decide where to hide the notice. He would have liked to destroy it, but when he came to the mouth of the disposall and opened it—letting the faintest, faintest whiff of the stink from the faraway incinerators mingle with the heady perfumes loading the air in the room—he found he had changed his mind. He needed the solid feel of it in his hand, the crinkly rustle of it in his ears, to drive him to the completion of his ultimate purpose.

During the party no hiding-place was likely to remain inviolate, especially in view of his reckless reputation, the guests would make it a point of honour to seek out and if possible ruin his most costly possessions, to make him break new records when he cleared up the mess and replaced the spoiled items. But he dared not have anyone even guess at the motive for throwing such a huge party on this randomly dated day. If anyone realised he had received his notice, the word would spread like the rumour of plague, and he would spend tonight alone, staring at nothing and feeling the cold hand of terror caress his heart.

"Oh, God *damn!*" he said aloud, snatching the notice into a place of concealment in the front of his loose silk shirt. Automatically he consulted his watch, though he knew the bell had rung twenty minutes ahead of party-time. It was the most expensive watch in the world; it had cost him four full years, and sat on the back of his left index-finger measuring the decay-rate of a minuscule grain of radium.

The bell sounded again. He reached his decision. What the hell point was there in keeping the notice? Every word of it was engraved on his mind, and could be summed into the single terrible warning: *tomorrow!*

But if he had no intention of being here, of even being alive, tomorrow—why hesitate to destroy a bit of paper?

He thrust the document into the disposall as he had originally intended. The gesture brought him a sense of calm, of boats being burnt. He went smoothly and coolly to open the door.

"You're early, but come in anyway. No reason to delay the . . ."

He got that far before he realised that the man facing him—a little older than himself, say thirty-five, slim, sat-urnine, bright-eyed—was wearing the black of an adult. And then, with a twisting grimace of disgust, he made to close the door, wishing it were possible to slam it with a crash.

"Wait," the visitor said softly. "Remember me, Hal?"

Page hesitated. He made a valiant effort to see the face above the drab black garb as that of an individual instead of merely as the mask of an anonymous adult, and relays of memory closed. He said, "Why, at a party of . . . What *was* the girl's name?"

"Karen Sottine—but that doesn't matter. Mine does. I'm Thomas Dobson." The man paused, his eyes as sharp as scalpels. "Well, are you going to make me stand here where anyone passing down the corridor might see me? Are you going to have people start to wonder why an adult comes calling on Hal Page, the professional youth? You see, I know about the notice you've had, and the reason for your spectacular party tonight."

"You're not going to be here?" Page forced out with violence. "I said 'open house,' but hell's name, I didn't mean—"

"No, of course not." Dobson managed to inject into the short disclaimer an infinite quantity of contempt, and Page wanted to writhe but lacked the time before the other continued: "Your guests won't be less than half an hour late; you know that as well as I do. Even for a glimpse of the legendary Hal Page who gambled and got away with it, who's dragging so many others after him by his example."

Page recovered his self-possession and made a mocking half-bow. "So it's for a sight of me that you've come, is it? To find out what you could have had, but missed? Well, come in, then! Have what you want at my expense!"

He waved Dobson past him with a grandiose gesture, indicating the array of delicacies with which the room was stocked; antiques and *objets d'art* had been thrust aside hastily to make room for them. "Champagne—genuine champagne from France? Caviar? Larks' tongues? I bet you've never had those! Take your pick, it's all charged to me!"

And added after a second, "But be quick!"

"Thank you," Dobson said, and selected a sliver of hard toast with which to dip into a bowl of red caviar. "You know," he added musingly when he had savoured the first mouthful, "it's a shame you can't value this for what it is—that you should see it only as a prop for your gigantic ego."

"But I enjoy it!" Page snapped. "And you're not

equipped to enjoy anything! Lord, even the first time I met you—what? Five years ago, must be—even then you weren't equipped to get any fun out of life! You sat there like a brooding ghost and poured out second-hand philosophical claptrap that nobody wanted to listen to—"

"You listened." Dobson dipped a second portion of the caviar and the toast crunched noisily between his teeth.

"Only because I didn't believe you could be real," Page grunted. "There you sat, and you went on and on talking though there was this pretty girl making eyes at you, the one with red hair and a mouth that . . . Well, skip it. But I got her afterwards."

"I know. She told me." Dobson swallowed the last of his toast and dropped into a soft chair. A fugitive smile crossed his face.

"You mean she looked at you twice?" A vague stab of non-comprehension troubled Page briefly.

"We got married," Dobson said. "A course of action which probably wouldn't appeal to you very much."

"Damned right," Page said shortly. "I've never let myself be trapped like that! She had a hell of a body, but her mind was all cluttered with the same kind of nonsense you were spouting all evening . . . And yet, you know, I guess I should be grateful to you in a way. Up to that time I'd run with the herd, I'd taken for granted all the pious nothings which I'd had spooned into my ears in school. I looked at you, and I thought *hell*, if they're going to take me and grind me into the same mould as you, I'm going to get my kicks first. And —why, yes! It was right on the following day that I went out and bought myself something that cost a whole year for the first time. And I felt great. And I kept right on going."

"Tell me something." Dobson cocked his saturnine head and regarded Page with apparently sincere interest.

"Didn't you feel anything when you ran your debt up over a century?"

"Sure!" Page uttered a harsh laugh. "I felt I was getting out from under."

"Nothing else?" Dobson probed.

"I know what you mean. You're trying to say: wasn't I scared that they'd come along and cut the ground from under my feet? Hell, no. You take yourselves too seriously, you adults. A minimum of thirty years' full free credit, that's what they tell you. Granted, I had a bad moment the day I woke up and found I was a week past thirty—I'd sort of lost count during a weekend party. But it kept on, and kept on, and here I am. Thirty-two years, one month and four days."

"Stop," said Dobson quietly, and reached for another dip of red caviar.

Page reddened. "So what's going to be done about it? My debt's up to three hundred years now, and there isn't a damned thing you can do! It's spent—or it will be by dawn tomorrow."

"And what do you have to show for it?"

"I have to show what anyone will tell you. I have proof of more guts than you. I have proof I wasn't scared of consequence. I didn't turn around and make myself into an adult ahead of the due date, so that when they called for me I'd go fawning and saying, 'Look, here I am already acting like one of you—please be kind to me!'"

A sudden thought broke his train of words like a derailment. He shot out an accusing finger. "Hey! How did you know about the—the . . . ?"

The question trailed off into silence coloured with more than a little alarm.

"No, I haven't come to drag you away by force, if that's what you're thinking," Dobson said equably. "My job is a little less demanding than that. I am in fact required to call on you and make sure you understand the responsibilities which go with the privileges you've enjoyed."

"Sure, I understand them fine," Page said, and motioned towards the door. "Now suppose you get on your way, and leave me to have my last fling."

"Sorry." The voice sounded genuinely regretful, but Page alertly sought a trace of sarcasm in the dark-browed face. "I have to do the job in a prescribed manner, and if I don't complete it before your guests arrive I shall just stick around until I have done it. So your choice is simple: sit and listen now, or sit and listen later, because there won't be anyone else here to keep you company. The news will have leaked out. And you know how superstitious everybody is in your group about a person who's been given notice. As though he suddenly carried the taint of a deadly disease."

That gibe penetrated Page's annoyance; earlier, he himself had mentally been comparing it to plague. He dropped into a chair facing Dobson and sighed.

"I'd rather take you and push your smug face down the disposall, but— Oh, spit it out and make it short!"

Dobson folded his hands calmly on his lap. He said, "I doubt if you've caught up on classics of literature during this expensive whirlwind of a life, but maybe if you'd done so you'd have developed greater insight into your situation, particularly if you'd read a couple of works by the dramatist Shaw. Early and mid-twentieth century. Mean anything to you?"

"Point! Come to the point! I've had my notice and I don't want to be *bored* tonight of all nights!"

"Ye-es, you have rather a marked capacity for boredom, don't you? Seems somehow unfair . . . Well, to be precise what I had in mind was a beautiful capsule summary of the contemporary economic setup which is probably apocryphal, but who can be sure? Reputedly Shaw said in his old age that youth was wonderful; what a pity it had to be wasted on the young! For in his view—as expounded at some length in *Back to Methuselah*—only the wisdom which age entrains can fit an individual to make optimum use of the energies of youth."

Dobson's eyes went once around the room, seeming to take in, sum up and dismiss everything for which Page had staked three centuries of existence. Page shivered and ordered him violently to hurry up with his little chat.

The other briskened. "All right. Well, even enclosed as you are in your psychologically incestuous circle of good-time chums, it must have been borne in on you that there has been progress since the old days? That we have colonised two other planets of this system, that we are reaching out to explore the planets of other stars?"

"I caught something about it on three-vee," Page said in a heavily ironical tone.

"Yes. Moreover we enjoy a universally high standard of living supported by a rational economic foundation to which we apply as the only truly dependable criterion of cost the investment of effort by the individual."

"I've spent three centuries' worth," Page grunted. "Have you any news that isn't stale?"

"Patience!" Dobson raised a slender hand. "I'm obliged to do this, as I told you. Even if your interruptions compel me to spend all night at it."

"I heard! I just don't see the point of the lecture on current affairs. Are you softening me up to tell me that I'm to be sent to Mars or somewhere to sweat on one of these damned construction projects?"

"You caught that on three-vee too, presumably," Dobson suggested with acid politeness. "No, you are not to be sent to Mars. The work there is almost at the stage where it can be automated, and only skilled options are likely to remain open there in future. Do I get the chance to make my point, or do you so much like the sound of your own voice you'd rather hear nothing else between now and tomorrow morning?"

Page made a disgusted gesture and leaned back in his chair.

"*Thank* you. In your last year of school when you should by rights have been old enough to make a fairly enlightened decision, you were instructed in the forms of modern society. You were told, for instance, of the expenditure against credit which would be made available to you at least until age thirty, and that the credit was charged like all expenditure nowadays against a standard base-scale of individual work. Only the time counts; there's no question, for instance, of someone who's not capable of highly skilled work being made to return more years of unskilled drudgery to balance the accounts. We're very rich as a species, we human beings—we don't have to be petty in such matters.

"You were told the reasoning behind this system. You were told—and like most adolescents you certainly didn't believe—that an endless round of pleasure and self-indulgence would ultimately grow boring, and that by the time you received your notice to repay to society the credit you had drawn, you'd wish to make some more constructive use of your life. You were told also that there was nothing rigid or compulsory about the obligation you were permitted to incur. There's a certain inalienable minimum available to everyone as long as he lives, so that by living frugally a person may if he likes continue to be his own master indefinitely. This course is usually chosen by those with a strong rebellious and creative bent, who would rather farm a plot of land on the edge of a desert and paint sunsets than take up an adult's regular post in society. I intend no criticisms of such people, by the way; the whole pattern of our evolution from the brute has centred on our ability to extend the period of play further and further into adult existence."

Unused to sitting and listening, Page had begun to

fidget. Now he burst out again, angrily this time, "I was certainly told all this, but I wasn't convinced, and I still am not convinced! I'm getting a hell of a lot of kicks out of life, and the idea of being arbitrarily grabbed by the neck and—"

"Not arbitrarily," Dobson cut in, with the first hint of strong feeling Page had yet seen from him. "You were told, even if you didn't pay attention."

"Told what? That—how did you put it? That an 'endless round of self-indulgence' would wind up by boring me? Hell, the only times I've been really bored have been like now, when some stuffy-brained adult started preaching at me!"

He jumped up and went to pour himself a shot of brandy.

"The fact remains," he continued over his shoulder, "I'm not fooled as easily as most people. You know they go around almost in *awe* of me? Like I'd done something special! All I did was see through this guff about 'my debt to society'! I told you frankly, I had some bad moments when I realised I'd hit age thirty with a debt already topping two centuries. Then I caught on. If you jumped on me right then and there, the first possible moment, the very day I got past the promised limit, you'd mark yourselves for scared. People would have said, 'It's a fraud! They served notice on Hal Page because he took what he wanted from life and didn't give a damn about the time they said he'd used up. Hell, if we're all going the same way in the end, let's take what we can while we can!' Isn't that the size of it?" He rounded on Dobson with a challenging glare.

"You're visualising the whole of your generation spending their credit by the century, the same as you," Dobson murmured. "Do you seriously think that would matter? I said we're a rich race. You have no conception how rich we are! We've learned how not to let anything go to waste—we had to, it was forced on us! If every single

one of the guests you've ever had to all your wild parties
—if every guest at every party you've ever been to—if
every member of your entire generation decided to spend
as freely and lavishly as you, all it would take to absorb
this would be to re-price their expenditure down to the
productive effort we can reasonably expect to require of
them during their later lives. We're embarrassingly rich,
Hal! These days, we seldom even have to send notices
to people. With the thirtieth birthday come and gone,
they tend to get restless—they tend to lose interest in
their round of pleasure—and they turn up one day and
ask to be assigned for some real work. I did that myself."

"But I'm not like you," Page rasped. Somehow the
contempt he had intended to load into his voice rang
false on utterance.

"The point I'm making still stands," Dobson countered.
"Our difficulty is in utilising the resources which make
themselves available to us. Nine people out of ten who
reach the age of thirty nowadays have already lost heart
for mere transient amusements; they've taken a course
of study, or set themselves a small research project, or
made plans for a family—done something adult, in short.
And we have to cope with this tremendous flow of creative energy, channel it, make the most of it . . . That's
why we're going out to the stars. It'll be a hell of a long
time before we actually reduce starflight to a routine
operation like a trip to the Moon, but we're going to
need that escape route simply for the sake of not wasting
the potential modern human society boils off like—like
surplus heat from an engine!"

"Finished?" Page growled. He drained his glass of
brandy and poured another shot.

"Not quite. We can't let things drift; that's what I'm
trying to put across to you. We can't raise the age of
full free credit to thirty-five, for example, simply to reduce the pressure on us to absorb the would-be adults."

"I'd have no objection!" blurted Page, thinking of the terrible warning he had thrust into the disposall: *Your full free credit period terminates tomorrow* . . .

"But already most people are finding it hard to last out thirty years fooling around." Dobson raised one eyebrow. "Did you not just hear me say so?"

"I've heard it all! I'm sick of it all! There's nothing more you can tell me—how about using the door?" Page tossed down the second brandy as though he hated the taste.

"Yes," Dobson sighed, and made to rise. "It's all been said to you, over and over. You just don't seem able to draw the necessary conclusions. 'None so deaf as those who will not—' Ah, never mind."

Page watched him move towards the exit. The hostility died in his eyes as the final question burned upwards into full awareness. Without intention, he found himself voicing it.

"Dobson! Do you know what's . . . ?"

And there it faltered, partly because he was ashamed to admit to this black-garbed intruder that the prospect made him afraid, and partly because he *was* afraid.

The saturnine man paused and looked back. "Do I know what they'll make you do? As a matter of fact, yes. But I'm not empowered to tell you."

"Make me? I thought there was supposed to be a range of free choice!" Page forced some of his normal bluster back into the words.

"You poor fool," Dobson said. "How many choices do you imagine remain open to someone who's spent more than three hundred years' worth of credit?"

And he was gone.

But it was a great party. There were just two bad moments—the first, when meditechs had to be called after a fight broke out between two men over some chit of a

girl Page had had last year and didn't think worth the
trouble; the second, when he found himself screaming at
the crowd to drink more, eat more, dance more frantically,
and realised that their faces were halfway frightened at
the intensity of his manner. He checked deliberately and
covered his moment of self-betrayal by seizing the nearest
girl around the waist to smother her face in kisses. He
must not—dare not—let it be suspected that he was under
sentence. Tonight, up to the very last minute, he must
be with people, he must have noise and laughter and
the crash and smash of priceless articles, a soft hot sweat-
pearled body under his, a silk pillow for his head ringing
with Dobson's calm terrifying voice in the echo-circuits
of memory.

With the third girl, around three in the morning, he
failed to make it, and knew that the time was come.

Abruptly he pushed her aside and got off the bed. He
went into the adjacent bathroom and shut the door behind
him; luckily there was no one in here now, though earlier three or four people had been showering down together and writing obscene verse on the walls with a bar
of lavender-coloured soap. He steadied himself with one
hand and gazed at his reflection in the floor-to-ceiling
mirror.

"Last time," he whispered. "But they'll remember me."

The one who cheated *them*. The only ambition he had
ever conceived.

It wasn't unique to himself. But others whom he'd heard
of, who had tried the same, who also found the prospect
of being snatched away from ceaseless selfish delight
intolerable, had botched the job. There were whispers;
there were shuddering rumours that followed casual ques-
tions. "Where's so-and-so lately? Haven't seen him
around." *Oh, he got his notice.* "And—?" *Tried to get
out from under. Cut his throat.* "And—?" *They healed
him.*

"I guess Dobson would approve of that," Page told his reflection, seeing grim lines form around his soft mouth. "I guess he'd say they were warned and had to take the consequences. But being told in advance doesn't justify it. I don't give a damn for paying back what I've had in credit. No one asked me when they set up this filthy system, and I opt out!"

His voice had peaked to a loudness which scared him; he didn't want to be overheard. When he left he wanted the party to continue. Maybe it would go on until the news came back: *Hal Page made it! Hal Page got out from under!*

One final twinge of irresolution overcame him; then he recalled the expression on Dobson's face as he went out, and thought about the implications of his parting promise.

No: better the silent dark of death. And he—he wasn't going to botch the job.

The aircar had cost him one and a half years of credit. It was going to be well worth it, he thought dreamily as he gulped down the five capsules of hypnotic —three hours' credit—and set the controls to carry him out to sea. There was just about enough fuel for fifty miles; by then he'd be at thirty thousand feet. And hitting water from such a height ought to be pretty much like smashing into a stone wall. If they even recovered enough to use for prosthetic grafts they'd be lucky, but that was the most they could hope to have back from . . . Hal Page's famous record-breaking debt . . . of more than . . . three hundred . . .

Blackness

And horror!

Light in darkness. Awareness. A shocking, horrifying lack of bodily presence. Vision, indestructible without lids to lower over the traitor eyes. He tried to scream, and found he had no voice; he tried to rise and run, and found he had no legs.

He was in a large light room, pale-walled, windowless, and facing him on a steel chair was the grim black form of Dobson, somehow elongated from front to back, as though he had become deeper since their last encounter. A voice said, "On now." A whitish presence moved at the edge of seeing, crazily out of proportion: a woman in a sterile coverall.

"I think you have the lenses too far apart," Dobson said. "He's probably getting exaggerated-stereo vision."

Something monstrous loomed close and the perspectives of the environment shrank to nearer normal. Hal Page seized on this inane consolation to divert his awareness from the unbearable central fact of existence: he wasn't dead!

"I'm sorry for you, Hal," Dobson said softly. "And by the way, don't try to talk. We haven't cut in the vocal circuits yet. We didn't expect to have to do all this to you at once, you see—it was your own fault for making that stupid suicide bid. Our plan was to take it slowly, cushion the shock."

The consciousness of Hal Page withdrew, turned into something smaller than a mouse, began to run frantically around and around in the confines of his brain . . . which, he knew and could not face knowing, was all that was left to him.

"You may go insane," Dobson said, his voice reduced to a thin whispering. "But I guess in some senses you've always been insane. Borderline psychopathic, incapable of drawing a rational conclusion from what you were told, incapable of empathising to the point of taking someone else's word. I guess, though, we have to be grateful that people like you still turn up occasionally . . .

"There was almost nothing left of you, Hal, but you

should have remembered what I said in your apartment: we don't let anything go to waste. We were great wasters once, we human beings; we learned the hard way what disasters waste could bring on us. Now we use foresight; now we make plans, and some of them are for a very long time ahead. We're compelled to be strictly honest —there are unpleasant tasks to undertake, and we never hide the fact. You elected yourself for one of them, in full possession of all the information which would have enabled you to back out if you'd chosen to. But you didn't. You went right ahead. You spent credit founded on other people's efforts until the free choices open to you as repayment dwindled to a single possibility. One year ago—two years ago—you could have paused and wondered why you were permitted to go on spending, spending, beyond any amount repayable in a normal lifetime. You never did.

"So here I am with the chore of explaining to you, after you made the mistake of thinking you could welsh on your debt." Dobson sighed heavily, his dark eyes scanning the complex array of prosthetics which kept the personality of Hal Page in being before him.

"We have to go to the stars, Hal. Creeping outward. As I told you, it's forced on us because we have so much energy to absorb, so much frantic creativity, so much skill and impatience. One day we'll go at the speed of light, freely and easily, but before that epoch arrives there must be scouts, explorers, pathfinders . . . You, Hal. You're going to Rigel, as the commander, and the crew, of a slow, slow rocket ship, and the round trip is going to last just about three hundred years."

EVEN CHANCE

Some of the fiercest fighting of World War II ebbed and flowed for months on either side of the territory of the Kalangs, but there was only one occasion on which the larger sweep of world events intruded into that inaccessible and hilly region of northern Burma to which they laid claim.

This intrusion began when a photo-reconnaissance plane on its way back from a risky but crucial mission suffered engine failure not far away. The pilot saw his navigator bale out safely, and shortly afterwards did the same himself. He wound up hanging from a high tree-branch in clear sight of a Kalang hunting-party, with sprains, scratches and bruises, but otherwise unharmed.

What little the hunters knew about either the white or the yellow man inclined them to distrust any stranger. However, the manner of the pilot's arrival—on white wings from the sky—was sufficiently impressive to prevent them acting on their first impulse and killing him out of hand. Instead, they escorted him at spear-point back to their village, where after duly consulting the omens the chief sheltered him, fed him and eased his pain with strong bowls of *ku,* which passes among the Kalangs for beer.

The plane, naturally, and the cameras it carried, were completely lost; however, the nature of the mission had been important enough for a search-party to go looking for survivors who might have verbal information. The pilot was found, feverish but alive. The officer in charge of the search for him very properly gave the Kalangs enormous gifts of tea, tobacco and salt.

When the strangers had gone, the chief fingered the beautiful steel of a machete which he had exacted as his own personal share of the reward and issued orders that anybody else who came floating down from the sky should be welcomed in the same fashion.

Tambah, of course, had not even been born at the time, but he had had this information as part of a long, complex, didactory tale his father told. He had seen the machete, a little rusted but still a thing to marvel at; he had seen the tattered ceremonial robe the chief of the time had caused to be made from the parachute, still worn on days of solemn celebration by his successor. To bring the now starving and depressed Kalangs such riches as the tale described—that had long been Tambah's most powerful ambition.

Even more powerful as a force directing his actions was his present anger. The chief had twice passed him over for the manhood ritual with contemptuous remarks about his small size, late sexual development and general incompetence. And that was why he had kept his great discovery to himself.

Not only that. He had set off to share it with other people—with strangers—before telling his own family. It was a fearful risk, and even though he knew the chance of anyone following him was minimal—since after much debate concerning recent unprecedented signs in the sky the whole tribe had settled down to a god-propitiating rite scheduled to last three full days—he could not keep from glancing over his shoulder every few minutes. He was tired and his feet were abominably sore; his burden grew heavier with each step he took. Yet he kept going,

lured by the dream of bringing the flying people to claim
their own and thus being the instrument of gaining new
riches for the Kalangs.

It was early morning when he came out of the thick
jungle and paused on an outcrop of rock, to see before
him a village of peculiar conical huts. For several seconds he did not take in their true nature; then he saw a
man emerge from one of them, and realised he had
reached his goal. He ought, he knew, to be cautious, but
somehow the reason would not come clear in his mind.
His thinking was blurred; the pain from his feet was dull
and unreal, and his mouth was very dry . . .

No: not completely dry. He sucked automatically at his
teeth, put up the back of the hand which was not steady-
ing his load, and wiped across his lips. When he took the
hand away there was a little smear of blood on the skin.

But his exhaustion forbade him to think even about
that. He stumbled down to the village of the flying people, trying to shout the news he had for them.

Jan Bailey walked around the jeep one final time to
make sure the cases of fragile ampoules were securely
lashed, rubbed a few flakes of mud off the World Health
Organisation insignia on the driver's door, and sighed.

"Seems okay," he muttered. "Think you'll find them today?"

"I guess we have a better chance than yesterday,"
Dinah Ashman said, glancing up from her counting of
hypodermic needles in the back of the vehicle. "We know
we're already inside Kalang territory now—we found that
abandoned village, for example."

"You're sure it was deliberately abandoned?" Carlos
countered from behind the wheel.

"We've been over that," Dinah snapped. "Yes, I am
sure! After all, it's a common enough pattern where you
hail from, or was a few centuries ago—clear some ground,

work it to death, move the whole tribe on to a fresh location."

Carlos scowled. Foreseeing an argument that might make for friction throughout the long day's expedition which lay ahead of the party, Jan ventured, "Look, I know this isn't my speciality, but . . . Consider: we know they're shy, and they've evaded contact with the outside world right up to the present, bar the occasional brush with soldiers during forty-three or forty-four. Could they not have heard rumours about our arrival and be hiding from us? Perhaps—oh, perhaps they took that giant meteor the other night as a warning from heaven about us."

"Then we'll just have to dig them out and persuade them we mean no harm," Dinah answered. "They don't keep themselves to themselves completely—if they did, we could afford to ignore them. But so long as they're a reservoir for yaws, any contact at all with anyone around is a damned nuisance."

"You, as they say in English, occupy the lifeboat," Ba Thway objected from his seat beside the driver. "Who shall have to do this persuading you speak of glibly? For a country with many ethnic groups in it America breeds damned few linguists."

"Can we save the argument until we're on the move?" Carlos grunted. "Or, better yet, until we return and can relax?"

"Yes, you have a hard day ahead," Jan said. "Don't worry, though. I'll spend any spare time I have praying for you to find your way back." He withdrew the sunburnt arm he had been leaning on the jeep door. Engaging the lower of the two differential gears, Carlos sent the jeep bumping over the rough ground.

Jan watched until it was out of sight. If ever they did locate these elusive Kalangs, he promised himself, he was going to take a couple of days off and help out with injections. When he first joined the WHO team he had felt rather sorry for them because their work was so repetitive: find a village, win the confidence of the people, vaccinate and inoculate them on a production-line basis, then move on and repeat the whole shtick. He had been sure his own project—a study of the local disease-vector pattern among water-breeding insects—was much more varied and interesting.

But now that it entailed him being left alone in the camp on four days out of five, he was getting distinctly bored.

And jumpy, too, he told himself when—some half hour or so later—he started and almost spilled a precious jarful of distilled water on seeing a flash at the corner of his eye, as though sunlight had glinted on a pane of glass. A second look showed no sign of movement in the vicinity; nonetheless he doggedly set off to investigate, first collecting—a bit shamefacedly—the expedition's only weapon, a twelve-bore shotgun.

From behind a rock a naked brown boy rose to meet him, carrying something large and shiny on his shoulder and dragging his feet as though intensely weary. At first he did not seem to notice Jan. When he did, he made to hold out the shiny object like an offering. The weight was too great. It slipped from his grasp and struck the ground with a metallic ring—and a moment later the boy keeled over in a dead faint.

Blazes! Jan stood perplexed, reviewing the half-dozen phrases he knew in Burmese—which almost certainly wasn't spoken hereabouts—and wishing the others were here. He had no knowledge of medicine beyond first-aid, and this boy was obviously very ill. He was covered in weals and scratches; his feet were cut and thorn-pricked; and because he was so thin it could be seen on his throat that his pulse was going like a hammer. Also a trickle of blood oozed from his mouth, no doubt, Jan reasoned, because he had cut his lip on falling.

Exhaustion combined with heat-stroke was the obvious diagnosis. Jan picked up the limp body and carried it to the nearest tent—Carlos'—where he set it down on a camp-bed. He attended to the abrasions and picked out the worst of the thorns, hoping that the boy might awaken of his own accord. When he did not, he brought a bucket of water and the largest bit of scrap cloth he could find, thinking vaguely of laying a cold compress on his forehead. Before doing so, he used the wet cloth to wipe the blood from the boy's chin.

That was when he began to wonder. The blood returned. On pushing back the lower lip he saw that the gums themselves were leaking a slow red stain. He gazed blankly for a moment, presumed pyorrhea in default of any better guess (wasn't there something about it being associated with endemic yaws?), and found a cottonwool swab and some antiseptic to wipe out the inside of the mouth with. The boy didn't stir, he was in complete coma now.

What could have reduced him to this state? Baffled, Jan left him after doing all he could and went to inspect the object he had been carrying, in the dim hope that it might offer a clue. It was a very strange thing to find in this remote corner of the world, but just suppose—well, perhaps it had fallen from an aircraft, struck the boy, hurt him, brought him furious out of the jungle to demand compensation . . . ?

No use making wild guesses. *Stick to facts,* Jan instructed himself, and turned the object over and over. It was all metal. By its lightness he hazarded that it was an aluminium-magnesium alloy. It had been formed to a precise curve, but one edge was jagged, as though an explosion had broken it away from whatever it belonged to. One side was discoloured—seemingly with the effects of intense heat.

Light though it was in relation to its size, he estimated

it would still tip a scale at around thirty pounds. Quite a load for a scrawny youth to tote through dense forest!

A new hypothesis replaced the former in his mind, that seemed a great deal more probable. There must have been a plane crash. The boy, wanting to report it but not knowing how to communicate with anyone outside his tribe, must have picked up this chunk of metal—to speak for itself, as it were—and travelled, perhaps for many scores of miles, until he came upon a white man. Yes, that would make excellent sense.

But there was precisely nothing Jan could do. He didn't speak the boy's language, and the boy was unfit to move, let alone show him the way to the crash, and the surrounding country was roadless, pathless, even trackless to anyone who hadn't been born and brought up here.

So he'd just have to wait out the day until the rest of the WHO party returned.

If they did. If they didn't locate the Kalangs and decide that having once found them they dared not let them out of sight until they had all been properly inoculated.

The logic of the conclusion he had reached was unquestionable, so he struggled to get on with his day's work. Concentration, though, turned out to be impossible. Every five or ten minutes he found he was impelled to peer into Carlos' tent. He knew it was pointless to do so, yet something nagging at the edge of his mind drew him back again and again.

Eventually, consulting his watch, he deliberately refrained for one full hour from going to see the same predictable sight. When the hour was up, he almost ran to the tent, so great was his accumulated eagerness.

The boy, without waking, had rolled on his side. Jan's first horrified impression was that he had thrown up black vomit, and visions of cholera filled his mind. Then the moment of gestalt seeing passed, and he realised that the dark stain on the pillow was a patch of hair which had come away from the scalp.

In the same moment he identified the nagging oddness which had kept teasing at his mind.

This tent belonged to Carlos. As well as being the expedition's driver and mechanic, he was in charge of their fallout monitoring kit. The latest of the test-ban agreements was in force, but modern techniques had brought the acquisition of nuclear weapons within the grasp of many small countries, and the Great Powers had laid so much emphasis on mass destruction as a status symbol that at any moment some new member might enter the portals of the Nuclear Club. Accordingly, every evening Carlos sampled the air and filled out a fresh line on a printed form, and each completed form was sent to the UN.

And right now, muffled by a covering of odds and ends under the bed, the Geiger counter in Carlos' kit was chuckling to itself.

Jan dug it out frantically. He swung the pickup, and as it traversed the limp body of the boy it rose to a scream before dropping back to a lower frequency with a change of scale; it was being triggered faster than the spring could re-set it at normal levels.

Sweating, moving with a kind of controlled panic, Jan went back outside. He improvised tongs from a couple of long sticks and with them carried the piece of metal well away from the camp despite complaints from his muscles due to having to cantilever such a weight so far from his body. He dumped it in a niche between two boulders which ought to afford some measure of shielding, and tossed the sticks down after it.

This was going to be hard on the boy, he reflected as he set a pan of water on the fire and hunted up a cake of disinfectant soap. But it would have to be done, hopeless though it probably was by now. And afterwards he'd have to scrub himself, pare his nails, change all his clothes . . .

Frantically he demanded of the unanswering air how a Burmese savage had come to suffer the worst case of radiation sickness he'd ever seen.

On their return that night—despondent at having failed to locate the elusive Kalang tribe—the others simply declined to believe him. Not until Carlos had checked the lump of metal with the counter were they convinced. And then they were as bewildered as Jan.

They could only hope that the boy might speak before he died; to that end, they checked his blood-group and discovered by a fortunate coincidence that it matched Ba Thway's. Dinah took charge of an emergency transfusion, and Jan and Carlos went back for another—very cautious—inspection of the lump of metal.

"What do you make of it?" Jan demanded.

Carlos hesitated. At last he said, "Frankly, it makes me wonder if we really did see a meteor the other night."

Jan pursed his lips. He knew, naturally, what Carlos was referring to, and had himself mentioned it this morning, the most memorable event of their expedition. They had all seen it, because it had happened after dark but before they turned in—a huge scything streak of flame across the night, followed by a roaring noise which according to Carlos' authoritative pronouncements implied that a large chunk of celestial debris had entered the lower atmosphere, a meteorite of exceptional size.

Jan pursed his lips. "I see! You mean . . . Well, I'm damned certain it couldn't have been an aircraft on fire, because I've seen two or three of those. What, then? You don't mean a missile with a nuclear warhead?"

"I'm not sure what I mean," Carlos muttered. "But in principle, no. To pick up a charge like this, a fragment of metal would have had to be so close to a fast reaction it would have melted, and I think this is too well engineered, too neatly shaped. In warheads you do not have reactions unless you mean the whole business. But consider an atomic engine."

A chill seemed to close on Jan's heart. He had heard, at second- or third-hand, from various colleagues that a breakthrough was imminent in that field, and everyone he had spoken to about it was terrified at the idea of radioactive material being sown broadcast through the stratosphere. He said, "Are you sure?"

Carlos shrugged. "Who can be sure about anything on the strength of a bit of scrap like that? But which is more likely to go wrong—a missile like thousands of others which have already been fired, or some craft with a nuclear engine, experimental? Come, let us go back. I want to speak to Rangoon."

The UN officials at Rangoon were likewise sceptical, all the more so because the transfusion had failed to revive the boy and the data the WHO team could pass were sketchy in the extreme. Nonetheless, a couple of hours after Carlos' initial report, a reply came through. The team were to stay put, and in the morning an aerial survey would be made of the locality.

"Ah!" Carlos said cynically. "What a quick reaction! It must be because the Burmese Army monitors all our calls."

Tired though they were, none of the party enjoyed much sleep that night. They took turns watching by the boy, and the rest of the time argued groundless theories around the fire. Carlos' hypothesis that a nuclear-propelled rocket might have crashed was uncomfortably convincing, and of course if they had stumbled on some well-kept secret of the Burmese government's they could look forward to deportation at best, or more likely an anonymous jail. On the other hand the thing that had crashed might have originated far away . . .

By dawn they were half convinced that Rangoon had made the promise of a search in order to shut them up for the time being. It was with mingled anxiety and relief that Jan spotted the first plane shortly after sunrise. His call brought the others running.

"High-altitude photographic plane," Carlos announced at length after studying it through binoculars. "A fat lot of use in this kind of country! By the time it gets back to base and the film aboard has been developed . . . Don't they have any helicopters?"

"Helicopters are slow," Ba Thway snapped. "How can they arrive so quickly as a plane?"

For a moment, hearing the sharpness of their voices, Jan was afraid that overtiredness might drive them to a shouting match; providentially, however, Dinah interrupted from the door of the tent where she was attending the boy.

"He's opened his eyes! Ba, come quickly!"

It was immensely difficult for Ba to piece together the boy's words. The local dialect—which they were shaken to find was the Kalang tongue, that of the very tribe they were seeking—was only a cousin of the languages he had studied, and the boy was on the edge of delirium most of the time. They did, though, learn that his name was Tambah, and that he was angry with his chief, and that there was some legend about a man from the sky, and that someone who told the flying people about a crash could expect to bring rich treasure to the Kalangs.

But at this point Ba began to doubt his own interpreting. For Tambah seemed to be implying that there was a man in the crashed aircraft, and that on the face of it was ridiculous. As Carlos commented, those countries sufficiently advanced to design a nuclear drive were also sufficiently advanced—and heedful of human life—to au-

tomate the control system. This surely must be wishful
thinking on Tambah's part; he must now be so confused,
the Mexican declared, as to be confusing the traditional
tale of a man from the sky with what he had personally
seen. Indeed, his behaviour supported the idea; he rolled
his eyes in fright whenever he was aware enough of his
surroundings to react to them, and all the time he
moaned his garbled pleas about being given a reward.

Ba gave him a reassuring pat on the chest and looked
at Dinah.

"How long will he last?" he whispered—ridiculously,
for the boy could not possibly understand English.

"If we can flag down a helicopter and transfer him to
a decent hospital, he may survive. If he's left here, he'll
die in a day or two. As a matter of fact I suspect he's past
hope anyhow."

"I'd better try and get a description of the crash site
out of him, then," Ba muttered. "You leave us alone. I
think I heard engines just now. See if that is a flight of
helicopters coming."

It was. But they continued past the camp-site, and did
not return until nearly noon, by which time the boy was
in coma again.

From the lead helicopter emerged an officer of the
Burmese Air Force, short, brown and plump, who informed them that he had been ordered to verify the existence of the mysterious piece of radioactive metal because
so far the photographic plane had not located any sign of
the crash. He also wanted more precise details of the
team's activities, and was politely contemptuous when he
learned that they had been tracking the Kalangs for
weeks without success, only to have a mere boy from that
very tribe locate them.

Just as he was concluding his interrogation more helicopters hove in sight: this time a full squadron, thirteen
strong. From then on, throughout the draggingly long

afternoon, they were never out of earshot of their beelike drone. Someone at high level, Jan thought, must be taking this seriously to put so many whirlybirds on the job. He said as much to Carlos.

Morosely the Mexican answered, "I could be wrong, you know. It doesn't *have* to be a chunk off an atomic engine that we have over there. It could equally well be a bit from a nuclear device that fizzled like a wet firework. Though if naked savages are building nuclear weapons now, all I can say is I want to get the hell away from the planet Earth."

It was almost sunset when the same officer as before returned. There had been no news for over two hours, as though someone had ordered radio silence to be imposed —for up to then they had caught odd snatches of chat between the searching planes.

Suddenly a swarm of helicopters passed near the camp. One of them had a big dark cradle slung between its undercarriage legs, while the others surrounded it above, below and on either side as though flying escort duty. The WHO team stood by their tents in puzzlement, wondering what that load might be.

Then the trailing 'copter detached itself and roared to a landing, and the officer descended from it, very pale and drawn. At first he seemed not to know what to say; finally he collected himself and stared at them as though at ghosts.

"I—I have some orders for you," he forced out. "At once return to your base. Not to use your radio under any circumstances, and not to tell anyone why you are going back without finishing your work."

"What?" As one, all the members of the team stepped forward.

"I . . ." The officer wiped his sweating face. "Oh, I tell you before I am forbid to! Listen! We find the plane that crash, scattered over mile of jungle. We find pilot, too."

Ba Thway exclaimed in wonder. "So Tambah wasn't delirious when he said there was a man in the thing!"

"No." The officer eyed him strangely. "No, he was wrong if say there was a man in it."

Jan was the only one of those listening who got the point. He felt all the blood drain from his face.

"You mean the pilot isn't a man?" he whispered.

"Okay right," the officer said. His eyes were on the dwindling silhouettes of the other helicopters. "They on their way to a hospital now, see if we can save him—I rather, see if we can save *it*."

"Oh God," Dinah said emptily, and then again: "Oh God."

"An atomic rocket," Carlos muttered. "With a creature in it from another planet . . . Oh, this is fantastic!"

"I see it," the officer said. "And what you say not so right either. Is in pieces, but you see for certain is not ordinary rocket. Something other."

"But with an atomic drive?" Carlos pressed. "Surely it must have an atomic drive, to make that piece of metal so hot!" He pointed across the camp-site.

The officer swallowed enormously. He said, "I think not so. We have Geiger counters, study outside of hull, then what we can of inside. And radiation is all on outside."

They waited. He hadn't finished confiding his terrible suspicions to them. At last, the decision to continue costing him dear so that perspiration stood in beads all over his face, he let them issue in a rush, his tone mirroring deep emotion.

"No, see, we find—find I think control-cabin, and then engine-part, and then what is—what must be—the guns."

Guns? Jan took half a pace forward, but the officer didn't notice, didn't interrupt the flow of his soft fearful words.

"All over one side, you see, metal soft with heat, gone splash. Same places always, tremendous radiation reading. I think ship crash here not by accident. I think . . ."

Now he did pause, and looked away from the vanishing helicopters to the darkling sky, where the first stars were winking into view.

"I think, somewhere up there, is war going on. I think that ship was shot down. And what I want to know is— who going to come look for survivors?"

The navigator of the reconnaissance plane baled out much earlier than the pilot, and landed a good twenty miles away. He reached the ground safely in full view of a village belonging to a people called the Ipoh, who knew almost as little as the Kalangs about the progress of World War II.

They were, however, a friendly and hospitable people, and greatly impressed by the manner of this man's arrival, on white wings from the sky. They gave him food and shelter, and when a search-party came to investigate from the nearest lines—where they had seen the parachute open—the navigator was found alive and well. The officer in charge very properly shot the chief for collaborating with the enemy and razed the village to the ground.

PLANETFALL

They saw each other at the same moment, and each failed to understand the expression on the other's face. The youth thought, "Why should she seem wistful? Or is it—? No! Surely she can't feel *bored!*" And the girl could not account for the look of wonder, unmistakable, which the youth wore.

Their faces changed. She smiled. He saw that and hesitantly smiled back. For long seconds neither moved. Then, absolutely without prior intention, she made a timid gesture at the ground beside her. His smile faded, returned, he began to look for a path to the top of the grassy knoll on which she sat, while she awaited his arrival with her heart hammering, hammering at her ribs until she thought it would break free and fly out like a small warm bird into the smoky afternoon air.

This was not something she had foreseen when she made her way out here, to this place giving a view clear across the untidy landscape surrounding the spaceport. From the knoll, highest point in sight by fifty feet or more, she could just discern the shallow concrete bowl of the landing-ground, dirty grey, with the five-mile tunnels of the transport system reaching out invisibly to the limit of local blast effect and there surfacing, as though the port's bowl were the dishlike blossom of some mon-

strous dry-land nenuphar extending blind roots in all directions. What she could not see, of course, was the
orbiting city, stationary overhead at twenty-three thousand miles or so, the other side of the shredded blue and
grey of the sky.

But it was that which had drawn her: not the prospect
of this or any meeting.

She had been astonished to see the boy wander into
sight so close to her. He wore the garb she had seen often
and often in pictures and on TV recordings—the plain
off-white coverall marked from every angle with symbols
that identified the wearer's exact function in the enclosed world of a flying city, on the chest, the back, the
buttocks and shins. He was tall and lean, clean-shaven,
with his scalp cropped close. Now, with head bent, he
was seeking sure footholds on the steep slope of the knoll,
and she realised she had not really noticed his face—
only a pattern of features matching the preconceptions
"male" and "young."

Knowledge of her own lack of perception started a flock
of associated ideas into consciousness, like a school of tiny
eager fish. How much had he actually seen her, from his
side? Had he perceived as little as she: a human form,
turquoise clothing, brown hair? Or . . . a pretty girl? She
did not go quite so far as to wonder whether he, from
space, would think of her as not-pretty, using a different
—alien—set of standards. But she did reflect that he might
speak only Russian, so that their communication would
be limited to a few halting words, and imagined frustration rose in her mind and became, on the instant, mad-
dening. This miracle opportunity, lost!

He was carrying something. She strained to see what it
was as he breasted the last rise and came into full view a
dozen paces distant. And it was nothing more than a
clump of wild plants, torn from the ground so that the

roots shed crumbs of dry earth, and crowned at the other end with a few drab would-be-blue flowers.

Lips parted, to utter words which refused to form, she stared. Now finally she did see his face, and was relieved. It was just a face: neither handsome nor ugly, having deep-set eyes, a long nose, a chin with a suspicion of weakness.

He said, driving away another cloud of futile anxiety, "Hello. Ah—my name is called Valeryk."

The frozen silence which had overcome the world without her noticing melted and was gone. She scrambled to her feet, pony-awkward, wishing she had grace instead of this limbs-everywhere adolescent clumsiness. "My— my name's Lucy! You're from the starship, aren't you?"

"Yes." And renewed silence, somehow reassuring this time, because during it she could tell herself that here was no superbeing, but a—well, a boy, perhaps eighteen or twenty at the most, uncertain what to say and do like any shy young stranger.

He turned, shading his eyes with the hand not holding the uprooted plants, to peer across the rolling off-green ground towards the port. "You can just see the ferry which brought me down, if you look carefully," he told her. He made each word separate, as though he were not sure how correct his pronunciation might be. "On the left, do you see?"

Eager, she stared, but could not tell which of the dark bulky forms fringing the bowl of the port might be a ship and which a building. Uniformly they were metal-grey, and the cloudy sky threw down from them no shadows to emphasise the distant shapes.

"Are you staying long on Earth?" she ventured. She had not seriously fantasised a meeting with a starman, in all the long hours she had passed here over the years, gazing at the inscrutable arch of heaven and thinking of other worlds, but the legacy of half-formed ideas related to such an encounter made her feel obscurely that it was wrong to spend this precious time in ordinary small talk. Yet nothing else offered itself to her tongue.

"We landed yesterday and must leave again tonight," Valeryk said. "But fortunately there has been a delay in the delivery of some supplies, and I have these hours to —to . . ." He made a vague gesture as though reaching into the air for an elusive word.

"To spare?" It was the best she could hit on: banal and uninspired. She railed against her own incapacity with words.

Valeryk laughed very quickly. There was no unkindness in the sound, but it did seem hollow, as though thought and not felt. He said, "Not exact. More to—to enjoy. To experience. To cram in."

To cram what in? The possibility that he would regard her as an interruption, an obstacle to some preformed plan, leapt up alarmingly in Lucy's mind. But she refused to pay heed to the idea. This was something she had never dared hope for, and she was not going to cut the conversation short.

"But you must have been to Earth before," she said. "You speak such beautiful English."

"No." He wasn't looking at her particularly; his eyes were everywhere, on the ground, on the sky, shifting almost greedily from one spot to another. "This is the first time I have ever seen the Home."

"But—ah—but the news reports said yours was a Russian city."

"It is, yes."

"Do you teach English in your—your schools?" Abruptly she discovered she had no inkling whether there were schools in the flying cities. But there must be some equivalent, the question could not sound too foolish.

"We have many kinds of people. We trade and exchange. Did you not know?" Valeryk turned a curious

gaze on her. She seized the chance gift of his attention
and shook her head vigorously.

"No, I don't know very much about life in the flying
cities. What's it like—really like?"

Valeryk shrugged. Already his eyes were roaming again.
"Monotone," he said. "These few hours of escape are
very precious."

Dismayed, Lucy cast around for some more concrete
question. So far she felt she was wasting time, and if he
was treasuring his brief freedom . . . The symbols on his
coverall sprang to her eye.

"These badges that you wear: what do they all mean?"

"Hm?" He shrugged up one shoulder as though to
give himself a view of the coloured shapes on his chest.
"Why, they say what is my position in the community.
The colour is brown to say I am apprentice; the upper
symbol is of a house and the under is of a blade of grass.
You would say ecologian. No, wrong. Ecologist."

He went on regarding the marks for several seconds
after he finished explaining them, and inspiration told
Lucy the reason. Here was something as much a part of
him as the nose on his face, and his conscious awareness
had been drawn to it for the first time in years. She said,
"You're given your jobs very young, aren't you? I'm sure
I heard, or maybe read—"

"Very young!" Valeryk's laugh was harsher this time.
"When I was five it was decided I and some others of like
age shall be ecologists."

A stab of envy provoked Lucy's next words. "It must be
wonderful!"

"What?"

"To—to *know*. To have a purpose all your life."

"I do not understand." Valeryk's brows drew together.

"It makes me envy you, it really does!" The words came
quicker now, she had tapped a source of emotion to power

them. "How old are you? Eighteen? Oh, forgive my asking, but—"

"Nineteen."

"So am I! But I don't know what I'm going to do—I don't know what my life is *for!* Everything's so *loose!* I could do a dozen different things, and there isn't any one of them where I'd know for sure I was being valuable to other people. I guess I'll probably settle for some time-wasting little job somewhere, when I get out of college, and then I'll get bored with it, and I'll meet some man and he'll persuade me to marry him and I'll have the permitted couple of kids and raise them—and then I'll be forty or forty-five and the kids will be independent and the guy will very likely be sick of the sight of me and I'll face another fifty years. With nothing."

Astonishment was bright in Valeryk's eyes at this outburst. "Nothing?" he exclaimed. "But you have—all this!" He swept his arms out to full stretch and embraced the world.

"I guess it doesn't look that way to you," Lucy admitted tonelessly. "To you all this is—I don't know—romantic? Exotic? Besides, didn't you call it the Home? But it is my home, and I don't care for what it offers me."

"How can you not?" He came a step closer. "Look! You said you envy me! Tell me why, tell me what you think I have that you do not!"

Challenged to put a nebulous sense of dissatisfaction into a neat package, Lucy was at a loss. Shrugging, she said, "I thought I did tell you. It's the same thing most Earth people—well, most young people, I guess—envy you starmen. The thing that makes us wait and wait by the TV when there's news of a flying city coming into the Solar System, and brings me out here to sit on the ground and just stare at the sky. I mean, I know I can't see your city except maybe at night if the sky's quite clear, and then all it is is a dot of light like any other star, not even moving because you go into this stationary orbit . . . But we wait, and hope and hope that it'll be our port you choose to orbit over and not one in Australia or Siberia or the Sahara. Because we want what you've got: the ability to know what use your life is going to be! You've known ever since you were five that you were going to be an ecologist for the city, a useful person, an indispensable person. I mean, I am right, aren't I? I must be right! Without ecologists you couldn't keep people alive in a starship. You make the whole marvellous thing possible!"

At first Valeryk had continued to frown over the incomprehensible passion that informed her voice. By degrees he had started to listen to what she was actually saying, and now he spoke in a serious tone.

"Yes—yes, it is true that without ecologists you could not plan for a starship's people, could not make it work. For I deal with food and water and air and the growing of the plants and the algae, and also the using of metals and salts and plastics and—and everything we have. Even the radiation we draw on for our power. Before I was permitted to come to Earth, I must help plot courses for solar accumulator ships we sent towards the orbit of Mercury. They are collecting energy to pull us out of solar gravitation before we turn on the interstellar ramjets and use the free hydrogen in quantities enough. That too is in my job."

"Well, then!" Heart aching to think that Valeryk was her own age and already so tightly knit with the community he belonged to.

But he gave another of his harsh little laughs. "What you do not see, little friend, is that I am *too* indispensable."

"I—I don't quite . . ."

"Is obvious." But there was no sarcasm in the comment. "Listen, and I shall try to make it clear. Because there are so many things involved in being ecologist, there

must always be too many of us. Almost anybody else has
a job where in emergency two can do the usual work of
three, and they will be tired out but the starship will
continue. An ecologist—no. We are permanently extended
to the limit. So there must always be too many of us. I
was chosen at five not because there were not enough,
but because there was a chance of one in two thousand
that when I was adult there might be a lack of an
ecologist. That was what the computers said: one in two
thousand chances. I am not for this purpose you so much
envy. I am for a chance which did not occur."

Bewildered, struggling as he had done to understand
the meaning behind the statement as well as the verbal
form of it, she said, "You mean there isn't any work for
you? But you just told me you were delayed by having
to work before they let you come down to see Earth."

"Oh yes, right now there is work for me. I am very
good at this job, I am intelligent and learn easily. So I
rather than another like me was called to attend this task.
But consider when I do not have work. What am I to do,
where am I to go? For me there is no hill of grass to sit
on, no place to go that I have not been to ten thousand
times. There is no *space*."

Lucy tried to object, but Valeryk plunged on.

"You would say there is any amount of it for me to
enjoy? Enjoy how? Shall I take a suit and go for a little
stroll—a million kilometres, perhaps?" Valeryk paused,
breathing heavily, his eyes fixed on her appalled face.
"Ah, I see you begin to understand. A little while ago,
you asked why I speak English. I said we trade and
exchange people. This is the reason why. I learned my
English from a girl—a woman now, she is married and
has twin babies—who came from one of your people's
ships." He hesitated, seeming to hunt for optimum words
again.

"Because . . . ?" Lucy was making a valiant effort to

put her own ideas into perspective, drawing on knowledge of the flying cities which she possessed but had
thrust to the back of her mind because it did not square
with her idealised visions. "Was it because there was a
shortage of men?"

"Hm? Oh yes, partly, I believe. And this is another
thing. I meet you and you are a stranger and it is wonderful! You are a new person, do you see? I have no strangers.
I have only friends and acquaintances. I meet strangers
when we trade crew with another ship. In my life to now
this has been four times. No, five. But the first was when
I was a tiny baby."

"Do you want to go to another city yourself?" Lucy
ventured, and was startled at the vigorous nod Valeryk
gave.

"But shall I ever get the chance? I'm an ecologist. If
I were in some other trade where the cities do not take
such care to plan a surplus of trained people, perhaps
I might hope. But why should ecologists be traded? Each
ship is unique, and I have learned my own, inside and
out, and no other. Perhaps if there has been some disaster,
some eco-catastrophe . . . But disaster may strike my
home as soon as any other."

He was staring at the horizon, narrow-eyed. "What
most of all I think I should do is leave. Stop here. Why
should I go back?"

The impact of his bitterness, so utterly different from
what Lucy had looked forward to, had now darkened
the girl's face as much as her mind, and he realised it
abruptly and took another pace towards her in dismay.

"But I make you sad!" he exclaimed. "Forgive me! You
should not be sad when you have so much that I wish
greatly for."

"Such as?" Lucy retorted.

"Why . . ." He suddenly recalled the clump of wild

plants still clutched in his hand, and thrust it towards her. "Why, that, to begin with!"

"It's only a weed," she muttered.

"Yes, to you it's 'only a weed,' but to me . . ." He fumbled desperately. "Look, don't you see? It has flowers. For no purpose of mine, or yours!"

"Don't you know what flowers are? Don't you have any in your city?"

"Of course we do, but for a purpose, a reason! I go around the plants and count the buds, decide how many will be needed for seed, cut off the others. They're the organs of reproduction, to be selected and fertilised and *used*."

"You complain that in your city you've been everywhere ten thousand times," Lucy countered stonily. "Well, I've seen those things ten thousand times."

Valeryk glanced at the now wilting stems and leaves, gave a hopeless shrug, and tossed the plant aside. The action seemed to cost him great effort.

"Very well, I accept the point. But—but colours! I stand here and turn my head, and suddenly from nowhere a bright gleam of colour, without design . . . That!" He shot out his arm. Among the leaves of a nearby bush, a smear of red.

"A can someone threw away," Lucy muttered. "Garbage. We make this whole planet a dump."

Valeryk, not listening, had gone to pick it up, come back turning it over and over in his hands. The paint was scored from its outside in random lines, and the protective layer of tin had gone with it, leaving the steel beneath to corrode.

"See? The shift of colour, the different—ah—*tints!* Not because someone planned it, not because a man came with a paint-spray and filled it in, but of its own accord."

"Not quite," Lucy said. "Because someone threw it

down, not caring whether it spoiled the place for other people. It could cut a child's leg. The edge is still sharp."

Blank, Valeryk let the can drop. "Then the air!" he suggested. "The air of which you have so much, not measured and metered, not recycled through a sterile machine!" He filled his lungs. "The scents, the smells!"

"Smoke," Lucy answered. "We're a good two miles from the town here, but that's what I can smell most of."

"But the wealth, the sheer wealth!" Valeryk exploded, almost dancing in frustration at his inability to make her see the point. "To have so much air you can let the smoke be there! I'm almost frightened by it! If I smell grass, or wet earth, or the odour of ripe fruit, I have to stop and think where I am, and if I'm not in hydroponics section I shout the alarm and run to see what's wrong in purification! All I may smell is—nothing. Only nothing is safe."

Dazed, she blinked and blinked at him.

"And the people in that town! And you yourself! So bored with the choices open to you." For the first time an edge of sarcasm did sharpen Valeryk's voice. "I say you cannot know what boredom is, with so much time on your hands, so many places to go, so many strangers to meet at no greater cost than walking along a street!"

"Yes, yes, but surely . . ." Lucy had to check and swallow to gain fresh purchase on the elusive words. "You must have free time occasionally, too. You must have"—this she had to force out—"girl friends. Surely you go out with them?"

"Hardly. I was not serious to speak of taking a suit and going for a stroll in space."

"You know what I mean!" Lucy could foresee her disappointment at the way this meeting with a starman was developing ultimately turning into personal dislike, and she had to repress the impulse to stamp her foot.

"You must have concerts, dancing, entertainment! Acting! Live acting, maybe?"

"Sure we do. What do you think we are waiting for, there at the port?"

"You said supplies—"

"But what kind of supplies? Have you never wondered why, after centuries and centuries, our ships have not been made self-sufficient? We are effectively a closed system when travelling between the stars, just as Earth is—this after all is a spaceship, carrying its billions through the void. Why go to the trouble of making planetfall? Why not eat the interstellar gas as whales eat plankton, process it up to complex elements, make our own carbon and oxygen and iron? Never venture closer to a sun than we need to go for extra stored power? Well, I shall tell you!"

His voice dropped. Without Lucy realising, it had grown late; the sun was close to the horizon and red stains were seeping out of the bank of cloud concealing the west. But it was not the cool of evening which made her shiver. Rather it was the intensity of Valeryk's voice.

"We are waiting for some music. For some poetry spools. For pictures, and carvings, and taped plays, and book-reels, and beyond that for recipes and—oh, for something to think and talk about!"

"But with a million people in your city," Lucy cried, "don't you have anyone who—?"

"A million? Where did you get that idea?"

Confused, she shook her head. "I always thought that by this time—"

"With a million, yes. It would probably be possible to isolate ourselves. Things might be random enough. Just. But what would a million people do plying between the stars, seeing maybe eight or a dozen planets in a lifetime?"

"Eight or a dozen!" The dying vision in her mind re-kindled. "You mean you may walk under a dozen different suns? Oh, that's marvellous!"

"Is it? To go out for a few hours when I gain senior rank, and can leave my underlings in charge of the work that is necessary in a solar gravitation field, worrying all the time for fear they should have made some mistake? Oh, if we did have a million . . . But we don't. Our population is about two and a half thousand."

"Then there are more people in my town than you've met in your life!"

"You're finally catching on," Valeryk said sombrely. His original hesitancy had vanished by now; he was speaking as rapidly and almost as fluently as Lucy.

"But they always talk of 'flying cities' . . ." The words trailed away.

"I have read in history about the reason. It was because at first there were ships that would support only perhaps a few scores of people. When they built the first of the very large ships, they said, 'We are sending a city to visit the stars.' The name has remained."

"Oh, I see." And after a brief empty pause she went on doggedly, "Even so, can't you make music of your own, write your own poems? Do you have to take all your art from somewhere else?"

"Oh, we have musical instruments, of course, for a little band, and . . . But perhaps I should tell you about Arkady Suslov. I never met him, but he is still famous although he went when I was about eight or nine."

"Went? Do you mean he died?"

"No . . . We were very proud of him in my ship. I guess we still are. You see, he wrote a play, and my father was one of the people who acted it, and they talked of it for years. Just the one play," he interpolated, correctly guessing at Lucy's unspoken question. "It was about—oh, it would be hard to explain it to you. About the argument which followed an accident in the power systems. A quarrel, with many accusations against the people supposed to be in charge.

"Like I say, we were very proud of him. When we raised other ships we reported this, flashed over a tape of the play being acted, asked if people on the other ship were going to act it too, and usually they said yes, of course we shall, it's something made by one of our people . . .

"Then time went by and with so much thinking about this, we all—I mean, everyone: I was still a child—everyone began to wonder where he had taken his ideas. There were so few sources. One of the characters was the . . . You say a villain, I think?" He cocked his head for her silent nod. "This villain, then, was a little like one person, and a little like another, and people worried more and more about the resemblances, and the idea of this accident affecting the power worried more and more people because although it was an accident of a kind which never had happened it was most convincingly possible, you see? There were special precautions taken to make sure it never actually would occur, and fewer and fewer people liked to talk to Suslov because they said he had not really made anything new after all, he had only made a rearrangement . . ."

"You said he 'went,'" Lucy prompted almost in a whisper.

"Yes." Valeryk seemed to come back from the very distant place to which his reminiscing had carried him. "We traded him off to another ship, which was delighted to have such a famous recruit—so delighted, I don't think they asked why we were anxious to be rid of him. And one hears occasionally he is most successful there, has written three more plays. Maybe they are well received because he can draw on people from my ship

for these new characters, and the people around him do
not suspect they recognise themselves."

There was a long silence once more, into which the
chill of approaching night stole, ghost-furtive. At length
Valeryk shook himself, almost like a dog emerging from
water, and turned to her.

"It is so strange that you should think we have a million people!"

"Well, they always say 'city'!" she repeated sullenly.
"And a million people isn't much for a city, you know."

"You think by Earthly standards. You have free air—
we must make ours and circulate it mechanically. You
have natural ground—we carry ours with us and must
tend it every second. You have the oceans—all our water
is in pipes and tanks. And ourselves." Valeryk made a
summing-up gesture. "We are an island. This is a continent."

"I see," Lucy confirmed slowly. "Is that why your—
your ships are so big? Of course it must be. And now I
understand why you said there was so much space here.
You mean waste space."

"And waste time, too," Valeryk concurred.

"I'm so sorry!" she cried. "Here I am keeping you talking, and you have only a few hours on Earth, and—
and maybe you will never come back!"

"Oh, don't mistake what I say. My English is not so
good, and when I said 'waste time' I did not mean
that here, now, I am wasting it. It is wonderful to have
this time with no duties to fill it! Here one can do nothing
for a day, a week even, and still he will live and breathe
and find food to eat. If I can see the Home only once
—you are right, in my lifetime we shall not be back—
what counts is to waste the time, throw it away. The
experience is unique. The smell of the air is unique, the
feel of the grass and the dirt under it, the colour of the
sunset . . ."

His voice trailed away as he turned and stared at the blurring reds and yellows marking the departure of the sun. Already Venus was just visible through a chance gap in the darkling clouds.

"What I lack," Valeryk said more to himself than Lucy, "is courage."

"What?"

"Courage," he emphasised. "If I had—there is a word I want . . . Ah! If I had *guts*, I would walk over the hill out of sight of the spaceport and never come back."

She sighed and put her hand out towards him. "Before you think of doing any such thing, you should come and see this Earth of ours."

He stood uncertainly, eying her outstretched arm. For a second puzzlement filled her.

"Do you not hold the hand of a girl when you keep her company in your city?"

"Yes, but . . ." She never learned what the *but* implied, for he closed his fingers on hers and came passively after her.

At the beginning he exclaimed over everything. To see dogs on the street excited him tremendously. "The wealth!" he breathed. "The richness of this place! Why, that one must weigh half as much as a man, and two such would consume his food, his drinking water, his air supply . . . And here they run in packs around the houses!"

Lucy said nothing, and he saw that the dogs were snuffling at garbage cans; then, how they visited the corners of walls, and how their soilings lay on the sidewalk and in the road.

Over the people at leisure to do as they liked, he exclaimed again, especially over those of his own age, free from the ceaseless obligation to worry about mere survival. That reaction lasted longer. Still she said nothing, waiting; then, when the night grew dark, shadowy figures sat on doorsteps and whined at them, begging money for liquor or drugs. That tarnished the glamour of idleness, and human stink displaced the remembered scent of wild grass.

The little things piled up. A fork had dirty stale food between its tines, from an environment where no bacterium was allowed to live without human permission, Valeryk squirmed on his seat and grew pale. The drink he chose was mere sweetened and coloured water with bubbles of CO_2 bursting in it; from a background where diet was controlled down to the last daily calorie he had to frown and try to assign this also to unlimited wealth. He failed. Moreover there was a woman at another table who kept sneezing, and he flinched every time and finally demanded why she was not in an isolation ward. To which Lucy said indifferently that it was just a cold.

A fight began outside a bar. From the other side of the street, still hand in hand, they watched. A crowd gathered. Its members stood by, not minded to interfere. On the contrary they shouted encouragement, and only scattered when a police siren announced the imminent descent of a patrol flyer.

Valeryk shook his head in bewilderment. "The—the waste of energy . . ." he began, and got no further.

Not without malice Lucy said, "Don't you fight among yourselves where you come from?"

"What for? How can we? The system depends—our very lives depend—on co-operative effort. This is one of the strange things about planetside dramas and stories which we pick up: this fantastic violence, this sense of surplus energy ready to boil off in new and unpredictable ways. But when it's reduced to *that* . . . !"

"You mean when it comes down to two drunks brawling on a streetcorner," Lucy supplemented, "it's not so attractive."

"No!" And then, as though reminded by the reference to picking up what he had earlier termed *supplies,* he started.

"What time is it, Lucy?"

It was the first time she had heard him use her name. She had half believed he had failed to catch it when she originally spoke it, and was too shy to ask for it again. The realisation of being wrong brought a curious, inexplicable thrill.

"Almost eleven," she said.

"I must be back at half past midnight."

"Then let's start walking now."

"It will not take an hour and a half to cover that distance, surely," he objected.

"Of course not." Lucy drew a deep breath, feeling her heart resume the violent pounding which had greeted Valeryk's initial appearance. "But let's go anyway."

Exactly as when she put out her hand to him, he hesitated, seeming to question the implications of her words. But now as then he acceded without voicing any opposition.

They left the town behind and were absorbed in the night, going cautiously because the ground was rough, still with hands linked, for a long time saying nothing. The clouds had blown over and the stars looked down out of more than half the sky. When they had walked for twenty minutes or so, far enough to bring them into view of the lights at the spaceport, Lucy ceased her formless speculations about what was going to happen and halted abruptly, raising her face to the stars.

"Can you tell which is your city, up in orbit?" she asked. Her voice was thin and quiet, to suit the empty dark.

Puzzled, Valeryk likewise gazed upward. He said, "No, I don't think so. I've never seen the stars from Earth before, remember."

"Are they so very different anywhere else you've been?"

"Why, yes! Down here under all this atmosphere there are very few, and I don't know which are simply rather bright and drive their light to the surface, and which must be new and out of place because it's my home."

"I never thought of that," Lucy confessed, turning her head away. "I thought you'd be able to locate the one which is a ship. I thought you'd—" She checked for a second, found she could not cancel the statement, however absurd it might seem. "I thought you'd point, and I could pretend to make a mistake and have to look upward along your arm, and lean against you, and . . ."

Her breath ran out into gusty nothingness.

There followed an eternal pause. During it Valeryk withdrew his hand from hers and began to link and unlink his fingers in front of his chest, over and over. When he spoke again it was in a changed voice, gruff and somehow older than himself.

"I'll tell you something too," he said, the words coming effortfully and at wide intervals. "I walked away from the port this afternoon, and my head was ringing with a million wild ideas. I thought, 'I can just walk and walk, and sooner or later I'll meet someone and get talking, and we'll be very friendly, and it won't have to be by conscious decision that I stay—it'll happen by itself because here at the Home there is so much to say, so much to think of, so much to do by choice and not from crude necessity.' That's what I was thinking. And of course I hoped most of all that the person I met"—he hesitated—"would be a beautiful girl.

"So when I came in sight of you and saw you smile at me, I felt . . . I felt disconnected. Between two worlds. Is it not the way with you, if something which has always been a fantasy suddenly turns into real life? I saw you like a flower on the hill, in that wonderful bright-coloured cloth, your hair like the natural earth itself,

brown and rich . . . I thought, 'It's going to be even
better, it's going to be incredible!' I . . . Oh, I guess I
should not say this, but I can't stop it, I must! I thought
the way it might work out would be that we'd—we'd
make love together, and it would be so good that I'd
never have to face the moment when I said to myself, 'If
I don't go back to the ship now, I remain on Earth.'"

"It could still happen," Lucy whispered.

"No."

The word had the finality of a cracking whip. In
horror she listened to its echo in her memory, and after
seconds had crawled by she felt a crawling on her
cheeks: two tears as irritating as insects.

She could hardly see Valeryk, but she knew he had
stopped working his hands back and forth and had
dropped them to his sides.

"I know you still want that," he said. "And you're
wondering what's to stop it. Let's lie down in the grass
and be together, and in an hour it will be too late, the
ferry will have lifted, they'll be making ready to call in
the accumulator ships . . . But—no."

"Why?" she quavered. "Why?"

"Because I came looking for flowers, and you rubbed
my nose in the dirt that grows them."

"It's true," she said at last. The tears had gone; there
were only those two, and now she felt hard and composed, as though a stone heart had been placed in her
breast. "And do you know why I did that?"

"I can guess," Valeryk said. But she would not let
him guess; she had to tell him.

"Because I envied what I thought was the purpose
and dedication of people like you. As you dreamed of
staying, not having to make a decision to change your
life but letting it overtake you, I thought of the way I'd
have been provided for if I'd been born into a starman's
family. I wouldn't have been condemned to agonies of

indecision, years of empty wondering about what I shall do with my life. You must understand, Valeryk! You hoped to—to slide around your decision, even the most crucial one you can ever hope to make. I have to make millions of decisions, all day and every day, and any single one can be so wrong that it leaves my life empty forever!"

Did he understand? She struggled to discern his face through the gloom. For a long time he did not answer, but finally he spoke.

"I thought you'd forgotten my name, or maybe not heard it clearly, and not wanted to ask me to repeat it."

And I thought . . .

"Oh, I'll never forget your name, Valeryk! I'll never forget *you!*"

"Nor I you. Because in spite of everything I have this— this weird feeling. I feel I ought to be so grateful to you."

He was rock-still for a moment; then he closed the gap between them in a single pace and brushed her cheek with his lips. Convulsively her eyes closed; convulsively she raised her arms to enfold him, and she held only the air. When she looked, his back was already turned and he was striding across the uneven ground towards the distant lights of the spaceport.

Next night, when she looked at the sky, it held one less star, but she never knew which star it had been that winked out and carried with it the ruin of so many dreams.

JUDAS

The Friday evening service was drawing to its close. The rays of the declining spring sun slanted through the polychrome plastic of the windows and lay along the floor of the central aisle like a pool of oil spilt on a wet road. On the polished steel of the altar a silver wheel spun continuously, glinting between two ever burning mercury vapour lamps; above it, silhouetted against the darkling eastern sky, there stood a statue of God. The surpliced choir was singing an anthem—"The Word Made Steel"—and the minister sat listening with his hand cupped under his chin, wondering if God had approved of the sermon he had just preached on the Second Coming.

Most of those in the large congregation were enraptured by the music. Only one man present, at the end of the rearmost row of bare steel pews, fidgeted impatiently, flexing the rubber pad from the forehead rest before him in nervous fingers. He had to keep his hands occupied, or they kept straying to the bulge in the inside pocket of his plain brown jacket. His watery blue eyes wandered restlessly along the climactic, sweeping lines of the metal temple and shifted away every time they came to the wheel motif which the architect—probably God himself—had incorporated wherever possible.

The anthem closed on a thrilling dissonance and the congregation knelt, their heads against the rubber rests, while the minister pronounced the Blessing of the Wheel. The man in brown wasn't really listening, but he caught a few phrases: "May he guide you in your appointed courses . . . serve as your eternal pivot . . . bring you at last to the peace of the true eternal round . . ."

Then he stood with the rest of them while the choir marched out to the strains of the electronic organ. Directly the minister had disappeared through the vestry door, the worshippers began to shuffle towards the main exits. He alone remained sitting in his pew.

He was not the sort of person one would look at twice. He had sandy hair and a worn, tired face; his teeth were stained and irregular, his clothes fitted badly, and his eyes were a fraction out of focus, as though he needed glasses. Plainly the service had not brought him peace of mind.

Eventually, when everybody else had gone, he stood up and replaced the rubber pad with scrupulous exactitude. For a moment his eyes closed and his lips moved silently, and as though this act had endowed him with the courage for a vital decision, he seemed to draw himself up like a diver poising on a high board. Abruptly he left the pew and walked—soundless on the rubber carpet of the nave—towards the small steel door that bore the legend *Vestry*.

Beside it there was a bell. He rang.

Shortly the door was opened by a junior acolyte, a youth in a grey robe woven of metallic links that jingled as he moved, hands in grey shiny gloves, scalp hidden under a smooth steel cap. In a voice made impersonal by careful practice, he said, "You wish counsel?"

The man in brown nodded, shifting a trifle from foot to foot. Through the doorway were visible many de-

votional pictures and statues; he dropped his gaze before them.

"What is your name?" the acolyte inquired.

"Karimov," said the man in brown. "Julius Karimov."

He tensed fractionally as he spoke, his eyes fleeting
over the acolyte's face in search of any reaction. None
showed, and he relaxed on the youth's curt order to
wait while he informed the minister.

The moment he was alone, Karimov crossed the vestry
and examined a painting on the far wall: Anson's "Immaculate Manufacture," depicting the legendary origin
of God—a bolt of lightning from heaven smiting an ingot
of virgin steel. It was excellently done, of course; the
artist's use of electroluminescent paint for the lightning,
in particular, was masterly. But from Karimov it provoked an expression of physical nausea, and after mere
seconds he had to turn away.

At length the minister entered in the officiating robe
of cobalt blue which identified him as one of the Eleven
Closest to God, his headpiece—which during the service
had concealed his shaven scalp—discarded, slender hands
playing with a jewelled emblem of the Wheel that hung
around his neck on a platinum chain. Karimov turned to
confront him, right hand slightly raised in a stillborn
gesture. It had been a calculated risk to give his real
name; he thought that it was probably still a secret, because Security had been fearfully efficient. But his real
face . . .

No, no hint of recognition. Shaving off his beard must
have turned the trick.

In his professionally resonant voice the minister said,
"What may I do for you, my son?"

The man in brown squared his shoulders and said
simply, "I want to see God."

With the resigned air of one well used to dealing with
requests of that sort, the minister sighed. "God is ex-

tremely busy, my son," he murmured. "He has the spiritual welfare of the entire human race to look after. Cannot I help you? Is there a particular problem on which you wish advice, or do you seek general divine guidance in programming your life?"

Karimov thought in horror: *Why, he believes! His faith is not pretence for profit—it's deep-seated honest trust. It's more terrifying than everything else that those who were with me at the beginning should believe.*

He said diffidently, "You are kind, Father, but I need more than mere advice. I have"—he stumbled at the word—"prayed much, and sought help from several counsellors, and still I have not attained the peace of the true round. Once, long ago, I had the privilege of seeing God in the steel; I wish to do so again, that's all. I have no doubt, of course, that he will remember me."

There was a long silence, during which the minister's dark eyes remained fixed on Karimov. Finally he said, "Remember you? Oh yes, he will certainly remember you! But *I* remember you too—now!"

His voice shook with uncontrollable fury, and he reached for a bell-pull on the wall.

Strength born of desperation poured through Karimov's scrawny frame. He hurled himself at the minister, striking aside the outstretched arm inches from its goal, bowling the tall man over, seizing the tough chain around his neck and pulling with every ounce of force he could muster.

The chain bit deep into pale flesh; as though possessed, Karimov tugged and tugged at it, twisted, took a fresh grip and tugged again. The minister's eyes bulged, mouth uttered loathsome formless grunts, fists beat at his attacker's arms—and grew weaker, and ceased.

Karimov drew back, shaking at what he had done, and compelled himself unsteadily to his feet. To the former colleague who now had gone beyond all hope of hearing he muttered his sick apology, then calmed himself with deep breaths and approached the door by which he had not entered the room.

On his throne beneath its wheel-shaped canopy of steel, God sat. His polished limbs gleamed under the muted lights; his head was beautifully designed to suggest a human face without possessing a single human feature—even eyes.

Blind insensate thing, thought Karimov as he shut the door. Reflexively he touched what he had in his pocket.

The voice too was more than humanly perfect, a deep pure tone as if an organ spoke. It said, "My son—"

And stopped.

Karimov gave an audible gasp of relief and his nervousness dropped from him like a cloak. He stepped forward casually and sat down in the central one of eleven chairs arranged in a parabola before the throne, while the blank shiny gaze of the robot rested on him and the whole metal frame locked in astonishment.

"Well?" Karimov challenged. "How do you like meeting somebody who doesn't believe in you for a change?"

The robot moved in human fashion, relaxing. Steel fingers linked under his chin while he reconsidered the intruder with interest instead of amazement. The voice rang out afresh.

"So it's you, Black!"

Karimov nodded with a faint smile. "That's what they used to call me in the old days. I used to think it was a silly affectation—assigning false names to scientists who worked on top-secret projects. But it's turned out to have advantages, for me at any rate. I gave my own name of Karimov to your—ah—late apostle outside, and it meant nothing to him. Speaking of real names, by the way: how long is it since anybody addressed you as A-Forty-Six?"

The robot jerked. "It is sacrilege to apply that term to me!"

"Sacrilege be—bothered. I'll go further and remind you what the *A* stands for. Android! An imitation of a man! A sexless insensate assembly of metal parts which I helped to design, and it calls itself God!" Scathing contempt rode the whiplash words. "You and your fantasies of the Immaculate Manufacture! Blasted by a bolt of divine lightning from a chunk of untooled steel! Talk about making man in God's own image—you're the 'God' who was made in man's!"

They had even incorporated the faculty of shrugging in their design, Karimov recalled with a start as the robot made use of it.

"Leaving sacrilege on one side for a moment, then," the machine said, "is there any valid reason why you should deny that I am God? Why should not the second Incarnation be an Inferration—in imperishable steel? As for your benighted belief that you created the metal part of me—which is anyway supremely unimportant since the spirit alone is eternal—it's long been said that a prophet is without honour in his own country, and since the Inferration took place at your experimental station . . . Well!"

Karimov laughed. "I'll be damned! I think you believe it yourself!"

"You are beyond question damned. Unless, that is, you renounce the error of your ways. For a moment I hoped, seeing you enter my throne-room, that you'd come to acknowledge my divinity at last. Of my infinite compassion I will give you one more chance to do so before my ministers take you away. Now or never, Black or Karimov or whatever you choose to call yourself: repent and believe!"

Karimov wasn't listening. He was staring past the shining machine into nowhere, while his hand caressed the bulge in his pocket. He said in a low voice, "I've plotted years for this moment—twenty years, ever since the day we turned you on and I began to suspect what we'd done. Not till now was there anything I could do. And in the meantime, while I sweated and hunted for a way to stop you, I've seen the ultimate humiliation of mankind.

"We've been slaves to our own creations since the first caveman forgot how to get his supper without a knife. After that there was no going back, and we built till our machines were so much more powerful than ourselves that we became terrified of them. We gave ourselves wheels when we might still have learned to run; we made airplanes when we might still have grown wings; and then the inevitable happened. We made a machine our God."

"And why not?" the robot boomed. "Can you name any way in which I am not your superior? I am stronger, more intelligent and more durable than a man. I have mental and physical powers that shame comparison. I feel no pain. I cannot fall sick. I am immortal and invulnerable and yet you say I am not God. Why? From perverseness!"

"No," said Karimov with terrible directness. "Because you are mad.

"You were the climax of a decade's work by our team: the dozen most brilliant living cyberneticists. Our dream was to create a mechanical analogue of a human being which could be programmed directly with intelligence drawn from the patterns in our own brains. In that we succeeded—far too well!

"I've had time enough in the past twenty years to work out where we went astray. It was my fault, God help me—the real God, if He exists, not you, you mechanical fraud! Always somewhere at the back of my mind while we were working on you there lurked the thought that to build the machine we had envisaged would be to become

as God: to make a creative intelligence, that none save
He had yet achieved! That was megalomania, and I'm
ashamed, but it *was* in my mind, and from mine it was
transferred to yours. No one knew of it; even I was afraid
to admit it to myself, for shame is a saving human grace.
But you! What could you know of shame, of self-restraint,
of empathy and love? Once implanted in your complex of
artificial neurones, that mania grew until it knew no
bounds, and . . . here you are. Insane with the lust for
divine glory! Why else the doctrine of the Word Made
Steel, and the image of the Wheel, the form that does not
occur in nature? Why else the trouble you go to in the
hope of making parallels between your godless existence
and that of the greatest Man who ever lived?"

Karimov was still speaking in the same low tone, but
his eyes were ablaze with hatred.

"You have no soul and you accuse me of sacrilege.
You're a collection of wires and transistors and you call
yourself God. Blasphemy! Only a man could become
God!"

The robot shifted with a clang of metal limbs and
said, "All this is not merely nonsense but a waste of my
valuable time. Is that all you came for—to rave at me?"

"No," said Karimov. "I came to switch you off."

At long last his hand dipped into the bulging pocket
and produced the object there concealed: a curious little
weapon less than six inches long. A short metal tube
extended forward from it; backward from the hand-
grip a flex disappeared inside his coat; under his thumb
there was a small red stud.

He said, "It took me twenty years to design and build
this. We chose steel for your body that only an atomic
bomb could destroy; how, though, could a man walk into
your presence with a nuclear weapon on his back, since
we gave you the power to detect radiation? I had to wait
until I had a means of cutting your steel as easily as a

knife cuts a man's weak flesh. Here it is—and now I can undo the wrong I did to humanity!"

He pressed the stud.

The robot, motionless until that moment as if incapable of believing that anyone could really wish to harm him, jolted upright, turned half around, and stood paralysed as a tiny hole appeared in the metal of his side. Steel began to form little drops around the hole; the surrounding area glowed red, and the drops flowed like water— or blood.

Karimov held the weapon steady, though it scorched his fingers. Sweat stood out on his forehead. Another half-minute, and the damage should be irreparable.

Behind him a door slammed open. He cursed, for his weapon would not work on a man. To the last possible second he kept it aimed, then he was seized from behind and pinioned, and the weapon was torn from its flex and hurled to the floor and stamped into ruin.

The robot did not move.

The tension of twenty hate-filled years broke and his relief boiled up into hysterical laughter which he fought to quell. When he finally succeeded, he saw that the man who held him was the junior acolyte who had admitted him to the vestry, and that there were other men present, strangers, gazing in utter silence at their god.

"Look at him, look at him!" Karimov crowed. "Your idol was nothing but a robot, and what men make they can destroy. He claimed to be invulnerable, but he lied! I've freed you! Don't you understand? *I've set you free!*"

But the acolyte wasn't paying him any attention. He stared fixedly at the monstrous metal doll, licking his lips, until at last he said in a voice that was neither relieved nor horrified, but only awed, "The Hole in the Side!"

A dream began to die in Karimov's mind. Numb, he watched the other men walk over to the robot and probe into the hole with instruments, heard one of them say, "How long to repair the damage?" and another reply offhandedly, "Oh, three days, I guess!" And it was clear to him what he had done.

Wasn't this a Friday, and in spring? Hadn't he himself known that the robot made careful parallels between his own career and that of the Man he parodied? Now it had reached the climax; there had been a death, and there would be a resurrection—on the third day . . .

And the grip of the Word Made Steel would never be broken.

In turn the men made the sign of the Wheel and departed, until one only remained. Stern, he came down from the throne to confront Karimov and address the acolyte who held him in a rigid grasp.

"Who is this servant of the devil?" he demanded.

The acolyte gazed at the limp figure slumped on the chair with the weight of all the ages crushing him, and replied, "Well, he calls himself Karimov. But of course he ought to say Iscariot."

Before the soundproof, germproof double glass window of the delivery room the matron of the maternity hospital came to a halt. "And there," she told the tall young American from the World Health Organisation, "is our patron saint."

Barry Chance blinked at her. She was a brisk fortyish Kashmiri woman with an aura of efficiency, not at all the sort of person one would expect to make jokes about her life's work. And indeed there had been no trace of jocularity in her tone. But in this teeming subcontinent of India a stranger could never be sure how seriously anybody took anything. After all, the universe was *maya*—illusory—according to the classical teaching.

He compromised. "I'm sorry," he lied. "I didn't catch that . . . ?"

Out of the corner of his eye he studied the man the matron had indicated. He was elderly and balding, what little hair remained to him had whitened into a sort of halo around his heavily lined face. Most Indians, the American had noticed, tended to grow fat with age, but this man had become scrawny, like Gandhi. Surely, though, an ascetic appearance and a halo of hair weren't enough to establish a claim to sainthood?

"Our patron saint," the matron repeated, sublimely un-

aware of her visitor's bewilderment. "Dr. Ananda Kotiwala. You're very fortunate to see him at work. It's his
last day here before he retires."

Struggling to make sense of her remarks, Chance stared
unashamedly at the old man. He felt his rudeness was ex-
cused by the fact that this corridor adjoining the delivery
room was a kind of public gallery. On every side there
were relatives and friends of the expectant mothers, down
to and including very small children, who had to stand on
tiptoe to peer in through the window. There was no such
thing as privacy in India unless you were rich. In any
overcrowded underdeveloped country a minute fraction
of the people enjoyed that luxury he'd taken for granted
since childhood.

The fact that toddlers could watch, fascinated, the arrival of their new brothers and sisters was accepted here
as a part of growing up. Chance reminded himself sternly
that he was a foreigner, and—what was more—a doctor
himself, trained at one of the few colleges that still administered the Hippocratic oath in full form to its gradu-
ates. He forced his personal preconceptions to the back of
his mind and concentrated on unravelling the curious
comment the matron had made.

The scene before him offered no hints. All he could see
was a typical Indian hospital delivery room, containing
thirty-six mothers in labour, of whom two were suffering
agonies and screaming—at least, to judge by their open
mouths and contorted bodies; the soundproofing was extremely good.

He wondered briefly how the Indians really felt about
their children entering the world under such circumstances. What it suggested to him was an assembly line,
the mothers reduced to machines producing their quota of
infants according to a pre-planned schedule. And all of
it so dreadfully public!

Again, though, he was falling into the trap of thinking

like a modern American, parochially. For untold generations most of mankind had been born publicly. Although
it had been estimated that the world's present living
population was just about equal in number to all the human beings there had ever been before the twenty-first
century, the majority of Earth's people continued that
ancient tradition, and made a birth a social event: in
villages, an excuse for a grand celebration, or here in the
city for a family outing to the hospital.

The modern attributes of the event were easily listed.
The behaviour of the mothers, for instance: one could tell
at a glance which of them had enjoyed up-to-date pre-
natal instruction, for their eyes were closed and their faces
bore expressions of determination. They knew what miracle was going on in their bodies, and they intended to
help it, not resist it. Good. Chance nodded approval. But
there remained the women who were screaming, no doubt
as much from terror as from actual pain . . .

He shifted his attention with an effort. After all, he was
supposed to be conducting a study of the methods in use
here.

The latest recommendations of the experts seemed to be
being properly applied—you'd expect as much in a large
city where most of the medical staff had had the benefit of
training abroad. Some time soon he was committed to going out into the villages, and things would be different
there, but he'd think about that when he had to.

The elderly doctor who had been called "our patron
saint" was just completing the delivery of a boy. Gloved
hand held up the latest recruit to the army of humanity,
glistening. A slap—correction: a beautifully restrained pat
with the open palm, enough to provoke a squall and the
first deep breath, not enough to aggravate the birth-
trauma. And handed over to the waiting nurse to be laid
on the little bench beside the bed, lower than the mother
so that the last few precious ounces of maternal blood

could seep down from the placenta before the cord was severed.

Excellent. All in accordance with the best modern practice. Except—why was the doctor having to explain so much so patiently to the awkward girl assisting him?

Chance's puzzlement was brief, then he realised. Of course. There weren't enough trained nurses in this country to allot one to every mother. So those girls standing neat and scared in their disposable plastic coveralls, their lank black hair bound in sterile plastic snoods, would be younger sisters or eldest daughters doing their best to help out.

Then the old man, with a final smile of reassurance, was leaving the worried girl and going to hold the hand of one of the women screaming.

Chance watched with approval as he soothed her, bringing about a complete relaxation within moments and—as far as could be guessed through the double barrier of soundproof glass and an incomprehensible language—instructing her how best to hasten the delivery. Yet there was nothing more here than he'd seen in a hundred hospitals.

He turned to the matron and asked directly, "Why do you call him 'patron saint'?"

"Dr. Kotiwala," the matron said, "is the most—now what would it be in English? Is there the word 'empathetic'?"

"From 'empathy'?" Chance frowned. "I don't know. But I get what you mean, anyway."

"Yes," the matron said. "Did you not see how he quieted the one who was screaming?"

Chance gave a slow nod. Yes, come to think of it, in a country like this, one could properly regard as a special gift the ability to break through the superstitious fright of a woman barely above peasant level and make her see what it had taken other women around her the full nine months of pregnancy and much skilled instruction

to understand. Now there was only one woman with her
mouth howling wide, and the doctor was soothing her
in turn. The other he'd just spoken to was yielding to her
contractions instead of fighting them.

"Dr. Kotiwala is wonderful," the matron went on.
"Everybody loves him. I have known parents consult
astrologers not to determine the most fortunate birthday
for their child but only to make sure it would be born
during Dr. Kotiwala's shift in the delivery room."

Shift? Oh yes: they operated a three-shift day. Once
more the image of the assembly line came to him. But it
was far too advanced a concept to reconcile with the idea
of applying to astrologers. What a crazy country! Chance
repressed a shiver and admitted to himself that he'd be
glad when he was allowed to return home.

For long moments after that he was silent, noticing
something he hadn't previously spotted: how, when the
labour pains permitted, the mothers opened their eyes
and hopefully followed Dr. Kotiwala's progress around
the room as though wanting to invite him to spend a
minute or two at their bedside.

This time their hopes weren't fulfilled. There was a
breeches presentation at the far end, and it would take
careful manipulation to reverse the baby. Plastic-clad, a
beautiful dark girl of about fifteen bent to watch what
the doctor was doing, putting out her right hand so that
the tense anxious mother could clasp it for comfort.

By his own standards, Chance thought, there was nothing remarkable about Kotiwala. He was obviously competent, and his patients appeared to like him, but he was
old and rather slow, and one could see how cautiously
he moved now the end of his shift was near and he was
tiring.

On the other hand, it was certainly admirable to find
the human touch in a birth factory like this. He'd asked
the matron, within minutes of his arrival, how long the

average stay of a patient might be, and she'd said with a wry smile, "Oh, twenty-four hours for the easy ones, and perhaps thirty-six if there are complications."

Looking at Dr. Kotiwala one might have assumed there was all the time in the world.

From an American standpoint even that didn't constitute a claim to sanctity, but through Indian eyes doubtless things looked different. The matron had warned him that he'd come at a busy time, nine months after a big spring religious festival which people regarded as auspicious for increasing their families. The warning hadn't prepared him for the reality; the hospital was *packed*.

Yet it could have been worse. He shuddered a little. The back of the problem was broken, but there were still something like 180,000 new mouths to feed every day. At the peak of the population explosion there had been just under a quarter million per day; then the impact of modern education was felt, people even in Asia, Africa and Latin America began to recognise the need to plan only for the children they could afford to feed, clothe and support while at school, and the crisis diminished.

Nonetheless it would be years before the children of that tidal wave of births could become teachers, workers, doctors to cope with the tremendous pressure. Thinking along these lines brought him to a subject which had been engaging a lot of his attention recently, and he spoke aloud without intending to.

"People like him, in this of all jobs—that's who they ought to choose!"

"I beg your pardon?" the matron said with positively British formality. The Raj had left ineradicable traces on the intellectuals of this country.

"Nothing," Chance muttered.

"But did you not say someone ought to choose Dr. Kotiwala for something?"

Annoyed with himself, yet—once reminded of the

dilemma shortly to be sprung on the world—unable to hold his tongue, Chance gave ground.

"You said it was Dr. Kotiwala's last day here, didn't you?"

"Why, yes. He retires tomorrow."

"You have someone lined up to replace him?"

The matron shook her head vigorously. "Oh, no! In the physical sense, yes, for another doctor will take his shifts, but men like Dr. Kotiwala are rare in any generation and in modern times most of all. We're dreadfully sorry to lose him."

"Has he—ah—passed the official retirement age?"

The matron smiled thinly. "In India we cannot afford the luxuries you Americans go in for, and that includes putting usable material—human or otherwise—on a scrap-heap before it's worn out."

With his eyes on the elderly doctor, who had success-fully reversed the breeches presentation and moved on to attend the woman in the next bed, Chance said, "In other words, he's retiring of his own accord."

"Yes."

"Why? Has he lost interest in his work?"

The matron was clearly shocked. "Of course not! Though I'm not sure I can make his reasons clear to you . . ." She bit her lip. "Well, he is very old now, and he does fear that some day soon a child may die be-cause he has let his attention wander. It would set him back many steps on the road to enlightenment if that happened."

Chance felt a surge of enlightenment himself. Believing he completely understood what the matron meant, he said under his breath, "In that case he damned well does deserve—"

And broke off, because strictly he ought not to be think-ing about this subject, let alone talking about it.

"I'm sorry?" the matron said, and when Chance shook

his head went on: "You see, when he was young Dr. Kotiwala was much influenced by the teachings of the Jains, to whom the taking of any life at all is repugnant. When his desire to cherish life led him to study as a doctor, he had to accept that some killing—of bacteria, for example—is inevitable to ensure human survival. But his kindliness remains founded upon religious principles, and it would be more than he could bear to think that his own arrogance in continuing to work when it was no longer safe had cost an innocent baby its chance to live a good and upright life."

"He can hardly actually be a Jain, then," Chance said, lacking any other comment for the moment. Privately he was thinking that if what the matron said was correct there were some old fossils back home, in medicine and in other fields, who could do with a transfusion of Kotiwala's humility instead of hanging on until they were dangerously senile.

"He's formally a Hindu, as are most of our people," the matron explained. "Though he tells me he has studied deeply in Buddhism too—which began, after all, as a Hindu heresy." She didn't sound greatly concerned. "But I'm afraid I still don't understand what you were referring to a moment ago," she added.

Chance thought of gigantic factories owned by Du-Pont, Bayer, Glaxo and heaven knew who else, labouring night and day with more expenditure of energy than a million mothers bringing forth commonplace human beings, and decided that the facts were going to be public knowledge soon enough for him to risk lifting a corner of the curtain of secrecy. It was depressing him to keep his mouth shut all the time.

He said, "Well, what I meant was that if I had any say in the matter people like him would get priority when it comes to—ah—the most advanced kinds of medical treatment. To preserve someone who is liked and admired seems better than saving someone who is mainly feared."

There was a pause.

"I think I follow you," the matron said at length. "I take it the anti-death pill is a success?"

Chance started. She gave another of her wry smiles.

"Oh, it's difficult for us to keep up with the literature when we work under such pressure, but there have been hints, haven't there? You in the rich countries like America and Russia have been trying for years to find a broad-spectrum specific against aging, and I think—knowing your countries by hearsay—that there must have been a long angry argument over who should benefit first."

Chance surrendered completely and gave a miserable nod. "Yes, there's a specific against senility. It isn't perfect, but pressure on the drug companies to put it into commercial production has grown so great that just before I left WHO Headquarters to come here I heard the contracts were being placed. A course of treatment will cost five or six thousand dollars and last for eight to ten years. I don't have to tell you what it'll mean. But if I had my way I'd pick someone like your Dr. Kotiwala to enjoy the results before all the stupid old men with power and wealth who are going to have their obsolete prejudices carried into the future by this breakthrough!"

He stopped short, alarmed at his own vehemence and hoping that none of the curious spectators surrounding them could speak English.

"Your attitude does you credit," the matron said. "But in one sense it's inexact to say Dr. Kotiwala is retiring. He might prefer to say he is changing his career. And if you offered to give him the anti-senility treatment I expect he would refuse."

"Why in the world—?"

"It is hard to make clear in English." The matron frowned. "You know perhaps what is a sunnyasi?"

Bewildered, Chance said, "One of those holy men I've seen around the place, wearing nothing but a loincloth and carrying a begging-bowl."

"And a staff, usually."

"A sort of fakir?"

"Not in the least. A sunnyasi is a man in the final stage of his life's work. He could have been anything previously —a businessman, commonly, or a civil servant, or a lawyer, or even a doctor."

"You mean your Dr. Kotiwala is going to throw away all his medical skills, all his experience, all the service he could still perform in this overcrowded country even if he did risk the life of a baby one of these days, and go out begging in a loincloth for the sake of his own salvation?"

"That is why we call him our patron saint," the matron said with an affectionate smile in Dr. Kotiwala's direction. "When he has gone from here and collected much virtue he will be a friend for us who remain behind."

Chance was appalled. A moment ago the matron had been saying that India could not afford to throw aside people with good work still before them; now here she was seeming to approve a plan that struck him as compounded of equal parts selfishness and superstition.

"Are you telling me he believes this nonsense about stacking up virtue for a future existence?"

The matron gave him a chill stare. "I think that is uncivil of you. The teaching of Hinduism is that the soul is born again, throughout an eternal cycle, until it achieves one-ness with the All. Can you not appreciate how a lifetime of work among the newly born makes all this real to us?"

"You believe it too?"

"That's irrelevant. But . . . I do witness miracles every time I admit a mother to this hospital. I witness how an animal act, a process with slimy, messy, *bloody* associations, brings about the growth of a reasoning being. I was born, and you, a squally helpless infant, and here we stand talking in abstract concepts. Maybe it is a mere function of chemical complexity, I don't know. I told you: I find it hard to keep up with the literature."

Chance stared through the window of the delivery room with a puzzled frown. He felt somehow disappointed—even cheated—after his near acceptance of Dr. Kotiwala on the matron's admiring terms. At last he muttered, "I guess maybe we'd better move on."

The sensation of which Dr. Kotiwala was chiefly aware was weariness. It went all through his body, to the marrow of his bones.

There was no hint of it in his outward behaviour, no suggestion that he was mechanically going through the motions. The mothers who committed themselves and their offspring to his care would have detected any such failing with perceptions deeper than ordinary, and he would have known the truth himself and felt he was betraying their trust.

But he was unspeakably, incredibly tired.

More than sixty years had passed since he graduated from medical school. There had been no change in the way human beings were created. Oh, the trappings had altered as medicine made its successive impacts; he remembered the inarguable disasters caused by drugs like thalidomide, and the upside-down blessings of antibiotics, that swamped countries like his own with more mouths than it could possibly feed, and now he was working with techniques which meant that nine out of ten of the children born under his supervision were wished-for, loved by their parents instead of being a burden or condemned to the half-life of illegitimacy.

Sometimes things turned out well, and sometimes badly. In the course of his long and valuable career Dr. Kotiwala had come to place reliance on no other principle.

Tomorrow . . .

His mind threatened to wander away from what he was doing: bringing to independent life the latest of all those he had delivered. How many thousands of mothers had moaned on the bed before him? He dared not count. And how many more thousands of new lives had he helped to launch? Those he less-than-dared to count. Perhaps he'd introduced to life a thief, an ingrate, a murderer, a fratricide . . .

No matter. Tomorrow—indeed, today, for his shift was over and this baby he was now raising by the feet was the last he would ever deliver in a hospital, though if he were appealed to in some miserable village he would doubtless help . . . Tomorrow there would be an end to worldly attachments. He would commit himself to the life of the spirit, and—

He checked. The woman alongside the mother, her sister-in-law, very much disturbed by the things she had had to do like sterilising her hands in disinfectant and stripping off her best sari in favour of a clammy plastic coverall, spoke a fearful question.

He hesitated over his answer. To the superficial glance nothing about the baby seemed amiss. It was a boy, physically whole, the usual flushed post-natal colour, letting out an acceptable scream to greet the world. All was as it should be. And yet . . .

He cradled the baby on his left arm while deftly raising first one, then the other eyelid. Sixty years of practice had made him gentle. He stared deep into the vacant light eyes, contrasting almost frighteningly with the skin around.

Beyond them was—was . . .

But what could one say of a child as new as this? He sighed and gave it into the care of the sister-in-law, and the clock on the wall ticked away the last seconds of his last shift.

Nonetheless his mind remained on the indefinable impulse which had compelled him to take a second look at the boy. When the doctor taking over from him arrived, Dr. Kotiwala concluded his summary briefing by saying, "And there's something odd about the boy just born in Bed Thirty-two. I can't put my finger on it. But if you get the chance, check him over, would you?"

"Will do," said the relief doctor, a fat young man from Benares with a shiny brown face and shiny soft hands.

The matter continued to irk Dr. Kotiwala even though he'd spoken about it. Changed, showered, ready to leave, he still lingered in the corridor to watch his colleague examining the baby as requested, making a thorough inspection from head to foot. He found nothing, and catching sight of Dr. Kotiwala as he turned away spread his hands and shrugged, his attitude implying, "Fuss about nothing if you ask me!"

Yet when I looked into those eyes, something behind them . . .

No, it was absurd. What could any adult hope to read in the eyes of a brand-new baby? Wasn't it a kind of arrogance that made him think his colleague was missing something of vital importance? In a dilemma, he considered the idea of going back into the delivery room and taking another look.

"Isn't that your patron saint standing there?" Chance muttered to the matron in a cynical tone.

"Why, so it is. How fortunate! Now you can make his acquaintance yourself, if you wish to."

"You've painted him in such glowing colours," Chance said dryly, "I feel I'd be wasting a chance if I didn't meet him before he forsakes the world."

The irony was lost on the matron. She bustled ahead with exclamations, but interrupted herself the moment she registered Kotiwala's glum expression.

"Doctor! Is something the matter?"

"I don't know," Kotiwala sighed. His English was good, but heavily accented in the singsong rhythm which the departed British had nicknamed "Bombay Welsh." "It is the child just born in Bed Thirty-two, a boy. I am *sure* something is wrong, but as for what it is I'm at a loss."

"In that case we must have him examined," the matron said briskly. Clearly she had implicit faith in Kotiwala's judgment.

"Dr. Banerji has checked him over and does not agree with me," Kotiwala countered.

In the matron's view Kotiwala was Kotiwala and Banerji was nobody; her expression said so louder than words. It struck Chance that here was his opportunity to find out whether the matron's admiration had any real basis.

"Look, rather than taking up more of Dr. Banerji's time —he has a lot to cope with in there—why don't you bring the child out and we'll take a look at him?"

"Dr. Chance, from WHO," the matron explained. Absently Dr. Kotiwala shook hands.

"Yes, that is a good idea. A second opinion, as they say. I'd welcome that."

It had been in the back of Chance's mind that his comparatively fresh training would enable him to apply some tests Kotiwala wasn't familiar with. In fact it was the other way around; the slow, thorough palping of the child's body and limbs, the delicate touching of the seven chakras, the traditional foci of the imaginary Yogic "vital force"—those were not in Chance's vocabulary of techniques. Of course, before the advent of modern instruments . . .

Anyway, valuable or not, such methods revealed nothing. Heart normal, blood-pressure average, all external appearances healthy, reflexes and vigorous, fontanelle a

trifle larger than normal but within normal range of varia-
tion . . .

After nearly three quarters of an hour, Chance was convinced the old man was doing this to make an impression,
and consequently was losing his temper by degrees. He
noticed that again and again Kotiwala rolled up the boy's
eyelids and stared into the eyes as though he could read
the brain behind them. On the latest repetition of the act
he snapped, "Tell me, Doctor! What do you see in his
eyes, hm?"

"What do *you* see?" Kotiwala countered, and motioned
for Chance to look also.

"Nothing," Chance grunted a moment later. They'd
checked the eyes, hadn't they, along with everything else?
The iris displayed a regular infantile reflex, the retinal
pattern was in no visible way abnormal.

"That's what I see also," Kotiwala said. "Nothing."

Oh, for pity's sake! Chance spun on his heel and went to
dump his sterile examination-gloves in the bin beside the
door. Over his shoulder he said, "Frankly I can't find anything wrong with the kid at all. What do you think could
be the trouble? The soul of an earthworm turned up in
his body by mistake, or something?"

Kotiwala could hardly have missed the scorn with
which the words were uttered, but his reply was perfectly calm and civil.

"No, Dr. Chance, I think that hardly likely. After a great
deal of contemplation I've come to the conclusion that the
traditional ideas are inaccurate. The human condition is
a human thing. It embraces the imbecile and the genius,
but it does not overlap with any other species. Who
could claim that the soul of a monkey, or a dog, is in-
ferior to that which looks out of the dirty windows of a
moron's eyes?"

"I certainly wouldn't," Chance said with sarcasm, and

began to peel off his gown. Kotiwala sighed, and shrugged, and was silent.

Later . . .

The sunnyasi Ananda Bhagat wore nothing more than a loincloth, owned nothing in all the world bar the begging-bowl and staff he carried. Around him—for it was cold in the hill country this bleak December—the people of the village shivered in their cheap coarse clothes, spending as much time as they could huddled over their tiny fires. They burned woodchips, rarely charcoal, and even now a great deal of cow dung. The foreign experts had told them to use dung for fertilizer, but the warmth of a fire was closer to the present than the mystery of fixed nitrogen and next year's crops.

Ignoring the chill, ignoring the strong smoke of the fire as it wandered upward and filled the gloomy hut, Ananda Bhagat spoke soothingly to a fearful girl of about seventeen, at whose breast a baby clung. He had looked into its eyes, and there he had seen—nothing.

It was not the first such in this village; it was not the first village where he had seen the same. He accepted that as a fact of existence. With the abandonment of the name Kotiwala had gone the preconceptions of a Doctor of Medicine, Trinity College Dublin, who had obeyed the behests of intellectualism in the sterile wards of a big city hospital. Throughout his eighty-five years he had sensed a greater reality looming over him, and his final decision had been to commit himself to it.

Now, as he gazed wonderingly into the empty face of the child, he heard a noise. The young mother heard it also, and cowered because it was loud and growing louder. So far had Ananda Bhagat come from his former world that he had to make a conscious effort before he identified it. A drone in the sky. A helicopter, a rarity here; why should a helicopter come to any particular one of India's seventy thousand villages?

The young mother whimpered. "Be still, my daughter," the sunnyasi said. "I will go and see what this is about."

He let her hand fall with a final comforting pat and went out of the misshapen doorway to stand on the cold windy street. The village had only one street. Shading his eyes with his thin hand, he peered upward into the sky.

Yes: a helicopter indeed, circling and glinting in the weak winter sunlight. It was descending, but that was not owing to his emergence into plain view. Before he recognised the sound of it, it must already have been coming down.

He waited.

In a little while the people came chattering out of their homes, wondering why the attention of the outer world in the form of this curious humming machine should be turned on them. Seeing that their marvellous visitor, the holy man, the sunnyasi—such as he were rare these days, and to be cherished—was standing firm, they drew courage from his example and likewise stood up boldly.

The helicopter settled in a blast of whirling dust, a little away from the beaten track called a street, and a man jumped down from it: a tall fair-skinned foreigner. He looked the scene over slowly, spotted the sunnyasi and let out an exclamation. Calling something to his companions, he began to stride up the street. Two others came down to stand beside the machine and talk in low tones: a slender young woman in a sari of blue and green, and a man in flying overalls, the pilot.

Clutching her baby to her, the young mother also came out to see what was going on, her first child—a toddler—pursuing her on unsteady feet with a hand outstretched to catch at her if his balance failed him.

"Dr. Kotiwala!" the man from the helicopter cried.

"I was," the sunnyasi agreed in a rusty voice. The

whole vocabulary of English had sloughed off his mind like a snake's overtight skin.

"For God's sake!" The man's voice was harsh. "We've had enough trouble finding you without your playing word games now we're here. Thirteen villages we've had to stop at on the way, picking up clues and being told you were here yesterday and moved on . . ."

He wiped his face with the back of his hand.

"My name's Barry Chance, in case you've forgotten me. We met at the hospital in—"

The sunnyasi interrupted. "I remember very well, thank you. But who am I, that you spend so much time and energy trying to trace me?"

"As far as we can tell, you're the first person ever to have recognised a Vitanul."

There was a silence. During it, Chance could almost see the sunnyasi's persona fading, that of Dr. Kotiwala replacing it. The change was reflected in the voice, which resumed its old "Bombay Welsh" rhythm on the next words.

"My Latin is negligible, for I only learned what was essential for medicine, but I take it that would be from *vita*, a life, and *nullus* . . . You mean: like this one here?" He gestured for the teen-age mother beside him to advance a pace, and rested his hand lightly on her baby's back.

Chance looked the infant over and at length shrugged. "If you say so," he muttered. "She's only about two months old, isn't she? So without tests . . ."

His voice trailed briefly away.

"Yes, without tests!" he burst out abruptly. "That's the point! Do you know what became of the boy you said had something wrong with him, the very last one you delivered before you—you *retired?*" There was monstrous fierceness in his voice, but it was not directed at the old

man he was talking to. It was simply an outward sign that
he had been driven to the limit of his resources.

"I have seen many others since," Kotiwala answered. It
was definitely not the sunnyasi speaking now, but the
trained doctor with a lifetime's experience behind him.
"I can therefore imagine. But tell me anyhow."

Chance gave him a look that reflected something close
to awe. The inquisitive villagers gathered nearby recognised the expression, and deduced—though not even the
best-educated among them could follow the rapid English
words—that the stranger from the sky was affected by
the aura of their holy man. They relaxed perceptibly.

"Well . . . Well, your friend the matron kept insisting
that if you'd said there was something wrong with him
there *must* be something wrong, although I'd said he was
okay, Dr. Banerji had said he was okay. She went on and
on about it until it was interfering with my work and de-
laying my departure. So I said to hell with it and had him
taken to WHO in Delhi for the most complete battery of
tests they could lay on. Can you guess what they found?"

Kotiwala rubbed his forehead wearily. "Total suppres-
sion of the alpha and theta rhythms?" he suggested.

"You did know!" The accusation in Chance's voice was
enough to shatter the barrier of language and communicate to the listening villagers, some of whom stepped
menacingly closer to the sunnyasi as though to defend
him if they had to.

Kotiwala bestowed on them a reassuring smile. He
said to Chance, "No, I didn't know. It just now came to
me what you would find."

"Then how in heaven's name did you—?"

"How did I guess the boy wasn't normal? I can't explain
that to you, Dr. Chance. It would take sixty years of work
in maternity hospitals, watching scores of babies being
born every day, to make you see what I saw."

Chance bit back a hot retort and let his shoulders

droop. "I'll have to accept that. But the fact remains: you did realise, within minutes of the kid being born, even though he looked healthy and none of our tests has ever revealed any organic deformity, that his brain was—was empty and there was no *mind* in it! Christ, the job I had convincing them at WHO that you'd really done it, and the weeks of argument before they'd let me come back to India and try to track you down!"

"Your tests," Kotiwala said, as though the last sentence had not been spoken. "Many of them?"

Chance threw his hands in the air. "Doctor, where the hell have you been these past two years?"

"Walking barefoot from small village to small village," Kotiwala said, deliberately taking the question in literal form. "I haven't followed news from the world outside. This is the world for these people." He indicated the rough street, the mean shacks, the ploughed and planted fields, the blue mountains closing all of it in.

Chance took a deep breath. "So you don't know and don't really care. Let me fill you in. Only a matter of weeks after I first saw you, the news broke which led to my recall from India: reports of a sudden appalling rise in congenital imbecility. Normally a child begins to react in at least a sketch for a human pattern while it's still very young. Precocious kids smile quickly, and any kid is likely to distinguish movement and colour, and reach out to grasp things, and— But I don't have to tell you!"

"Except these you have named Vitanuls?"

"Exactly!" Chance clenched his fists as though trying to seize something out of the air. "No life! None of the normal reactions! Absence of normal cerebral waves when you test them on the EEG, as though everything that makes a person human has been—has been left out!"

He levelled a challenging arm at Kotiwala's chest. "And you recognised the very first one of all! Tell me how!"

"Patience." Bowed by the weight of all his years, Kotiwala still held himself with immense dignity. "This in-
crease in imbeciles—it struck you directly after I retired
from the hospital?"

"No, of course not."

"Why 'of course'?"

"We were too tied up with . . . Oh, you've been out
of touch, haven't you?" Chance spoke with bitter sarcasm.
"A minor triumph of medicine was making all the head-
lines, and giving WHO enough headaches to be going on
with. The anti-senility treatment had been made public
a few days after I saw you, and everybody and his uncle
was standing on line yelling for it."

"I see," Kotiwala said, and his aged shoulders finally
hunched into a posture of despair.

"You see? What's that supposed to mean?"

"Forgive my interrupting. Continue, please."

Chance shivered, apparently as much at what he was
remembering, as at the bite of the air. "We'd done our
best, and postponed announcement of the treatment until
enough was stockpiled to treat several million applicants,
but of course that was as bad as breaking the news at the
lab stage, because everybody's best friend seemed to have
died last Friday and here were people screaming that
we'd killed them by neglect, and— Hell, you get the picture. Whichever way we handled it, it came out wrong.

"And then shovelled on top of that mess came the new
one. Congenital imbecility hits ten per cent of births,
twenty, thirty! What's going on? Everyone spins in little
circles because just as we were congratulating ourselves
on sorting out the row about the anti-senility treatment,
here comes the most fantastic crisis in history and it's not
going to break, it's going to get worse, and *worse* . . .
Over the past two weeks the rate has topped eighty per
cent. Do you understand that, or are you so sunk in your
superstitions it doesn't bother you any longer? Out of

every ten children born last week, no matter in what country or continent, eight are *mindless animals!*"

"And you think the one we examined together was the very first?" Kotiwala disregarded the harshness of the younger man's words, his eyes were staring, unfocused, into the blue distance over the mountains.

"As far as we can work it out." Chance spread his hands. "At any rate, when we checked back we found the first kids of which this had been reported had been born on that particular day, and I happened to remember that the time of birth of the earliest we'd heard about was an hour or so before I met you."

"What happened on that day?"

"Nothing that could account for it. Every resource of the UN has been put to work; we've sifted the world's records to the very bottom, and not for that day only but for the time nine months earlier when the kids must have been conceived—only that doesn't fit either, because some of them were preemies as much as six weeks early, and they're the same, hollow, drained . . . If we weren't at the end of our tether, I'd never have done such a crazy thing as coming to look for you. Because after all I guess there isn't anything you can do to help, is there?"

The fire of rage which had burned in Chance when he arrived had turned to ashes now, and he seemed to have no more words. Kotiwala stood thinking for a minute or more, and the villagers, growing restless, chattered among themselves.

At last the ex-doctor said, "The anti-senility drug—it's a success?"

"Oh, yes. Thank God. If we didn't have some consolation in the midst of this mess I think we'd all go crazy. We've cut the death rate fantastically—I told you we had enough for millions of people in store before we published the news, and because we planned well we can hope to feed the surplus mouths, and . . ." He broke off. Kotiwala was staring at him strangely.

"Then," the old man declared, "I think I can tell you what happened on the day we met."

Dazed, Chance took half a pace forward. "Out with it, then! You're my last hope—you're *our* last hope."

"I can't offer hope, my friend." A sound like the echo of doom's own knell coloured the words. "But I can make what they call an educated guess. Did I not read once a calculation which showed that as many people are alive in this twenty-first century as have ever lived since the evolution of human beings?"

"Why yes. I saw that myself, a long time back."

"Then I say that what happened on the day we met was this: the number of all the human beings there have ever been was exceeded for the very first time."

Chance shook his head in bewilderment. "I don't see! Or—or do I?"

"And it so turns out," Kotiwala continued, "that at the same time or very shortly afterward, you find, and make available the world over, a drug which cures old age. Dr. Chance, you will not accept this, because I remember you made a kind of joke about an earthworm, but I do. I say that you have made me understand what I saw when I looked into the eyes of that new-born child, what I see again when I look at this little girl here." He touched the arm of the young mother at his side, and she gave him a shy quick smile.

"Not the lack of a mind, as you have been saying. But the lack of a soul."

For a few seconds Chance imagined that he heard the hollow laughter of demons in the whisper of the winter wind. With a violent effort he rid himself of the delusion.

"No, that's absurd. You can't mean to maintain that we've run short of human souls, as though they were

stored up in some cosmic warehouse and issued off the
shelf every time a child is born! Oh, come now, Doctor
—you're an educated man, and this is the rankest kind of
superstitious rubbish!"

"As you say," Kotiwala agreed politely. "That is something I won't venture to dispute with you. But I owe you
my thanks, anyhow. You've shown me what I must do."

"That's great," Chance said. "Just great. Here I come
half across the world hoping that you'll tell me what to
do, and instead . . . What? What must you do?" A final
flicker of hope leapt up in his face.

"I must die," said the sunnyasi, and took his staff and
his bowl, and without another word to anyone, even the
young mother whom he had been comforting when
Chance arrived, he set off with slow old-man's paces along
the road that led to the tall blue mountains and the eternal ice, by whose aid it was lawful for him to set free his
soul.

FACTSHEET SIX

Mervyn Grey, nicknamed the Boy Wonder of the Business World, had not become a millionaire at twenty-nine through indecisiveness. Accordingly, when he found an overnight memo sent by teleprinter from Edgar Casson, his London deputy, which said Casson counted himself fortunate to have obtained thirty pence a share for holdings in a company which a week ago had been quoted at ninety-six, he left the Grand Bahama headquarters of his financial empire on the next VC-10.

He hadn't bothered to send ahead and say he was coming, but the stolid, heavy-set broker was not surprised when a chauffeur-driven Rolls halted before his expensive home that evening. He told his wife to entertain the dinner guests on her own, to keep his food warm for later, and not to interrupt him on any account, and himself welcomed Grey in the library.

Short, blond, tense to the point of feverishness, always seeming—even when sitting behind his desk—to be on the point of heading elsewhere at a dead run, Grey dropped into the most comfortable chair, took the fuller of the two glasses of sherry which Casson poured, and demanded, "What in hell's name happened to Lupton and White?"

Casson had been anticipating this, but as usual having

the width of the Atlantic between them had given him an exaggerated impression of his ability to deal calmly with Grey in a bad temper. He licked his lips nervously and said in a defensive tone, "It's still happening, you know. They went through sixpence by close of business this afternoon and tomorrow you won't be able to give them away. In the circumstances I think it was creditable to—"

"*What happened?*" Grey barked. "And give me another glass of that muck you were conned into buying as sherry."

Casson complied with a sigh. Much of the day he had been mentally rehearsing the explanations he was going to offer if Grey turned up, and with considerable polishing he felt he had prepared a rather impressive story: the initial astonishment, the quick reaction which shaved their losses, the discreet pumping of knowledgeable acquaintances, the eventual remarkable discovery . . .

But the hell with it. If he prevaricated, Grey would quite likely fire him. He set down the newly filled glass with a shrug and reached into the inner pocket of his impeccable dinner-jacket.

"*That* happened to them," he said baldly, and thrust a sheet of paper, folded twice, into Grey's outstretched hand.

"*Factsheet Five,*" Grey read aloud from the heading. "What does this have to do with it?"

"Read the whole thing," Casson muttered. "Then you'll know almost as much as I do, or anyone else I've spoken to."

Grey scowled, but complied. What he had been given was a sort of leaflet, produced by photo-offset from a typed original—a badly typed original, moreover, with irregular margins, many errors and even two or three lines which had been crudely x'ed out. The heading was in bold black Letraset capitals, but even that was a sloppy job and the capital F of "Five" was creased at the top.

Altogether there were about ten or a dozen short paragraphs, each prefaced with the name of a company, of which he recognised the majority. With growing anger and bewilderment he read through them.

DALE, DOCKERY & PETRONELLI LTD. Ice-cream and ice-lolly manufacturers. During the last six months 3,021 children who had bought their products contracted stomach disorders.

GRAND INTERNATIONAL TOBACCO CORP. "Prestige," "Chilimenth" and "Cachet" cigarettes. 4,186 of the cases of lung cancer diagnosed last year occurred among users of these brands.

SCIENTIFICALLY TESTED PROTECTIVES LTD. Surgical rubber goods. 20,512 unwanted pregnancies occurred last year in cases where the parents had relied exclusively on the firm's products.

And there was the one he'd been looking for: *LUPTON & WHITE LTD. Caterer's equipment. 127 employees of firms using bread-slicers, bacon-slicers and other cutting devices supplied by this company lost one or more fingers in the period under review.*

Grey winced and shuddered at the momentary image of a hand spouting blood across the clean white enamel of a bacon-slicer, but he had a fifty-thousand-pound loss on his mind. He looked up at Casson, who had taken a chair facing him and was gloomily piercing a cigar.

"This—this *rag* did for Lupton and White?"

"So I've been told," Casson confirmed.

"But for heaven's sake!" Grey counted rapidly on both sides of the paper. "There are eleven companies named here. Did anything happen to the others? How about Grand International Tobacco?"

"They launched a new promotion scheme two weeks ago which had already significantly increased their sales. It started an upward trend in their price, too. In the normal course of events you'd expect that to continue for about half a year. But for whatever reason the trend levelled off yesterday and today they slipped back three-pence. I agree, that isn't evidence. But the coincidence is indicative."

"Oh, for the Lord's sake! That happens all the time, that kind of thing, and a nosedive like Lupton and White's is practically unprecedented unless the accounts show probable bankruptcy! How can you argue that a slovenly scrap of paper like this is responsible? And in any case why this firm in particular, instead of the contraceptive makers with twenty thousand alleged victims?"

"I concede that Lupton and White were far from headed into bankruptcy. Last year's profits were up eight per cent on the year before, their P/E ratio is still about right, and . . . But you can't get back at a firm that lands you with an unwanted baby. You can, however, sue someone who cost you a finger, and there's this new Industrial Compensation Bill going before Parliament, isn't there?"

Grey drew his brows together. "I see! You mean the clause which will try and extend liability to the manufacturer of goods that don't comply with the British Standard. They'll never get it through, of course—we're going to see to that—but I can imagine people being scared . . . Not as scared as all that, though!"

"Not everyone is as certain as you are that the bill will be amended," Casson said. "And I've been doing some calculations. If this figure is correct, and if similar cases can be taken as a guide, then if the performance of last year were to be repeated, Lupton and White could be hit for something around three million quid in damage claims."

"They'll just have to re-tool to meet the standard, then,"

Grey snapped. "It'll cost them . . . Oh. I remember. They re-designed their entire line three years ago, didn't they?"

"And still haven't paid off more than sixty per cent of the loan they obtained to finance the job." Casson gave the words an air of finality. "No, confidence in Lupton and White is nil, and they can look forward to going through the floor. Which is, I suppose, a kind of poetic justice, assuming their gadgets really did injure all these people."

"Nonsense!" Grey exclaimed. "Any idiot should know that a sharp cutting-instrument is dangerous! So's a pocketknife—so's a razor-blade, come to that."

Casson's mouth twisted as though he were amused despite his depression. "The person who puts out that Factsheet is fully aware of that," he said. "You haven't read the second side, have you? Look at—I think it's the last item but one."

Grey turned the paper over. He read aloud, "New Dawn razor-blades were used in twenty-three of the twenty-eight face-slashing cases known to the police in—" And, breaking off abruptly, he stared at Casson.

"How in the world could anyone take this rubbish seriously? There must be a lunatic behind it!"

"Someone took it seriously. A lot of people, in fact. The proof lies in what happened to Lupton and White, doesn't it?"

"Proof? You can't call that proof!" Grey jumped up and began to pace the room. "What about all these other companies? I didn't see a simultaneous crash by all of them!"

"Three of them aren't public companies, so they can be disregarded, and in fact one wonders why the compiler of the sheet included them. And the rest are subsidiaries of much larger combines, which can cushion the blow."

"But—!" Grey slammed fist into palm furiously, and the

Factsheet floated to the floor. Casson bent and recovered it.

"But what?"

"But granting that you're right, something ought to be done about it. Isn't this—well—libel or something?"

"I'm afraid not. You can't libel a corporation, only an individual."

"But it's such transparent nonsense!" Grey thundered. "Who in heaven's name could track down the parents of all these unwanted babies? It's absurd!"

"Absurd or not, I assure you it's taken very seriously by a lot of people. Shall I explain?"

"Yes, go ahead." Grey slumped wearily back into his chair.

"It took me a lot of probing to get hold of that issue of the Factsheet," Casson said. "I called—well, let's say a long-time friend of mine—while I was trying to find out what had happened to Lupton's, and he said if he'd realised I had a holding in the firm he'd have tipped me off. I asked how he knew, and he said he'd tell me if I had lunch with him, which I did, and that was when he showed me that paper. He told me he had photostats so I was welcome to keep it.

"He said he doesn't know anyone else who receives it, and he has no idea why he gets it or who sends it to him. It simply arrives, roughly once a month, in a plain envelope and always with a different postmark. He's been reading it since issue number three, which he thought was a crank's ravings and threw away. However, one item did stick in his memory because it referred to a canned-meat company he was interested in, and implied they were lax in their hygiene. So, superstitiously—to quote his own term—he revised his intention of buying in. A few days later an outbreak of typhoid in Leeds was traced to canned corned beef shipped by that very firm. Naturally, the bottom dropped out of their sales for three months until the impact of the news faded."

"Go on," Grey said, listening intently.

"Well, next time he received a Factsheet, of course, he read it very carefully. He had no holdings in any of the firms it listed, but he kept an eye on them out of curiosity. One of the entries was similar to this one here, about the ice cream, and said a lot of children had fallen ill after buying toys imported by Kid-Dee Fun. You know them?"

"Of course. Dolls and novelties from Hong Kong and Japan. And they were the people who ran foul of Consumers' Association."

"Correct." Casson nodded. "There proved to be an arsenical compound in the paint used on some of their toys, and they had to call in ten thousand pounds' worth and burn them."

"Who the hell was it who told you all this?" Grey demanded.

"He asked me not to give his name to anyone," Casson murmured. "But . . . Well, let me just say that I'm far too cynical to swallow a tale like this without verifying the teller's credentials, as it were, so I made some discreet inquiries. He's turned the twenty thousand he was left when he was twenty-one into something more like a million and a half, so I'm prepared to certify his competence and judgment."

Grey looked at him for a long moment. He said finally, "Has this Factsheet fellow ever gone for any of the really big companies?"

"I don't know."

"Let me see that leaflet again!" Grey snatched at it and pondered in silence for a while. At length he said, "I have to give the guy credit. He's smart, isn't he?"

"How do you mean?"

"Oh, come off it!" Grey snorted. "It'd be obvious if you could see beyond the end of your nose! This is a brilliant con job, put out by one of the cleverest market manipulators I ever heard of. There's a pattern here, though, which gives him away. You honestly don't see it?"

The nervousness which Casson thought he had escaped by convincing Grey of the truth of his assertions returned in full force. Feebly he shook his head.

"In that case you're more gullible than I imagined," Grey snapped. "Maybe I should think about handing over my affairs to someone who isn't soft in the head with premature senility! Goddamn it, man, work it out! From what you've told me all these sheets follow a similar pattern. Each includes a kernel of hard fact—the infected meat in one issue, the arsenical paint in another—which could be established by anyone with access to the right channels. I'll bet I could compile off the top of my head a list of twenty damaging facts which I could use against as many different companies with household brandnames. Then I could invent lots more, dressed up with statistics which could neither be verified nor disproved but which would take colour from their surroundings. And I'll bet that's what he's doing, whoever he is. And *then* I could salt the whole lot with an item about a company which is peculiarly vulnerable owing to special circumstances, like Lupton and White. Result: the ultimate in inside market information, the self-fulfilling prophecy."

Casson said, "Yes, but—"

"But what? Oh, come on, come on! What's your opinion of the person who puts this collection of nonsense together?"

"Well—"

"A public benefactor, drawing attention to products which make people ill, chop their fingers off, kill them in accidents? In that case why doesn't he attack big companies with staff who could follow up his charges? Directly or indirectly I control a labour force of sixty thousand, don't I? I could hire a hundred more tomorrow if I had to, checking out the claim that umpty-dozen cars riding on Ultrac Tyres were involved in accidents last month, or however many housewives were drowned in Miracle Whirl washing machines." Grey gave a harsh laugh. "That's why he doesn't go for the big boys. They could prove him a liar if they had to."

"And would you?" Casson said.

"Would I what?"

"Would you hire the people to check the claims? When the CA car-testers reported that Ultracs skidded more easily and were more likely to come away from the rim of the wheel when cornering at speed—"

"I did sweet Fanny Adams about it. Correct. How in hell could you expect me to? Any tyre will misbehave if you treat it badly enough. And we weren't wiped out, were we? Of course not. Sales went *up!* Ultracs have massive appeal because they're cheap and well advertised. All this consumer-testing nonsense affects maybe a hundred thousand buyers in this whole country, and there are millions over and beyond those few who want what I'm giving them. These are hard commercial facts, aren't they? I didn't invent the market, and no more can I be held responsible for the people it consists of. But you haven't answered my question: did you honestly picture the publisher of this Factsheet as a knight in shining armour, crusading against dangerous consumer goods? No, you couldn't be *that* naïve."

Hideously embarrassed, Casson felt himself begin to flush under the lashing scorn of the younger man's tongue. He was fifty-four. Not for the first time he wondered how much longer he could stand working for this—this *youth*. When they first met he had been exactly twice Grey's age. He was experienced, successful, highly regarded in his own field. Yet there was something about Grey which could make him cringe, want to curl up inside himself and go a long way away very quickly. Perhaps

it was what the admiring gossip columnists had no hesita-
tion about terming ruthlessness; perhaps it was just that
his unashamed greed made him acutely sensitive to the
greed of the people who bought the products he offered.

His career had begun with household durables, and the
discovery—not novel, but never previously regarded in
the light Mervyn Grey shed on it—that people resented
having to pay so much for the equipment to perform un-
glamorous chores like the laundry, yet felt forced to ac-
quire high-priced high-precision equipment for them because that act itself loaned the work a smidgin of glamour.

That led to knocked-down washing machines, assem-
bled in half an hour with the help of a screwdriver—supplied. The result was not merely handsome—he hired good
designers to package his products, good market-research-
ers to find out what colour, trim and "extras" were most
desirable—but big. For the investment of thirty-odd minutes of your time, you could have a machine the size
of those owned by neighbours who had paid three times
as much as you. What was more, yours was prettier.

From there he went on to other expensive items for the
home, likewise in kit form, and having exhausted the possibilities there—TV was out of the range that interested
him—he turned to the next highest item in the family
budget, the car. First there were trimmings to make a
routine vehicle look like a custom-built modification,
and then there was the major breakthrough into the tyre
business, following the discovery that drivers resented
having to pay so much for equipment no one but experts
would notice and compliment them about, and would
rather fit a sun-visor and a windtone horn than a new suit
of high-performance tyres.

And so on, in a fantastic pyramid. There had been
nothing like it since John Bloom's meteoric rise, and un-
like his predecessor Mervyn Grey showed no sign of
overreaching himself. Even a disastrous loss like the one

he had just suffered through Lupton & White would appear as a minor debit in the balance sheet of a holding
company worth ten times as much.

What next?

Casson grew aware that Grey was staring at him sar-
donically, and fished back in memory for the echo of the
last thing that had been said to him.

"Well—ah, no! I don't suppose I did picture this fellow
as a 'crusader.'" Recovering rapidly from his moment of
dismay, he ploughed on. "On the other hand, he must
have a bee in his bonnet, don't you think? I've been assuming he suffers from misplaced idealism."

Grey considered the suggestion, his expression becom-
ing more cordial. "I think not, though it is a rational possibility. A monomaniac obsessed with things like road
safety, the health of children and so on, would be more
likely to let fly wildly—at the biggest corporations, as I
said before. No, this has all the earmarks of a cunning,
thoroughly planned campaign. So let's take advantage of
it."

He leaned back in his chair and put his fingertips together. "I want you to do two things. First, buy Lupton
and White."

"What? But they're headed for bankruptcy!"

"Blockhead! I don't mean pick up their surplus shares
for wallpaper! I mean sweep up a good fat majority holding and add the company to our list! Who financed their
restyling the other year—wasn't it one of the merchant
banks? Well, it doesn't matter, but whoever did it won't
want the company to go bust. They'll become the effec-
tive controllers of what assets survive, and if the property
won't cover their outlay they'll listen to a scheme for recovery, won't they? This new Industrial Compensation
Bill won't become law next week, for heaven's sake! We
can dump any dangerous products—export 'em at cost if
we have to. There's bound to be some ignorant nignog

somewhere who'd like to pretty up his jungle grocery-store with a nice new slicing machine! Hell, why should I have to spell out the details to you of all people? A change of title and the magic of the name 'Mervyn Grey,' and we can have the firm back where it was inside a couple of years. All that's wrong is that you panicked and dropped our holding, so now we're going to have to buy it back, aren't we?"

Casson said, "But when it started to slide so fast—"

"You stuck to rigid principles instead of using a bit of imagination. Ah, never mind. At least we'll pick up what we let go at a fraction of the old price. With luck we'll come out with a profit after all. But you're going to have to sharpen up a bit, you know, Cassie-boy."

"Don't call me that!" Casson snapped.

"Why not?" Grey's tone was a savage caress. "When you behave like an inexperienced teen-ager, can I help thinking of you as years my junior? Shut up, anyway, because I don't want to spend longer than I can help in this chilly damp country. The other thing you're going to have to do to make up for your mistake is find me the person who publishes that." He stabbed his finger through the air towards the Factsheet. "He's got something going for him. I'd like to have it going for me. Never let it be said that I can't recognise an original idea, especially when it pays this kind of conspicuous dividend."

He rose and headed for the door. "You've got until the next issue comes out, Cassie-boy," he threw over his shoulder. "Otherwise you're through. 'Bye!"

The more Grey thought about it, the more he was impressed with the brilliant simplicity of the Factsheet idea. If, in the space of a few short months, the man behind it had built up such a fund of confidence as to take in Casson—who, for all Grey's gibes, was extremely competent—and Casson's anonymous friend, and at least several score people with substantial holdings in Lupton & White, since otherwise the price slide would not have been so swift or so complete . . . then he had a remarkable gift for exploiting gullibility. It was Grey's lifetime conviction that the mass of the world's population were both greedy and extremely stupid. Finding someone else who had reached the same conclusion and benefitted from his insight was enough to make him decide that he and the person in question belonged to the élite.

Day by day little snippets of data arrived across the ocean from London which enabled him to round out his picture of the mysterious market manipulator. At first he had been inclined to expect that Casson would eventually unmask the identity of someone he already knew about—he was far from the only entrepreneur who could profit from picking up a catering-equipment company dirt-cheap. As time passed, however, he began to think of the unknown as a financial counterpart of a gypsy fortune-teller, not merely because he employed the standard technique of slipping in the crucial item among a fog of carefully selected irrelevancies and endowed the whole with a phoney air of precision by tabulating those incredible statistics, but also because of the ingenious misdirection he had adopted from the start when presenting his monthly bulletins.

If he had issued something slick and professional, people would at once have associated him with the regular market-information agencies. Instead, he had taken the risk of having his material dismissed as the drivel of an incompetent amateur and banked on luck supplying him with a small hard core of people who had read some single item closely enough to remember where they had seen the prediction when it was fulfilled. With Casson's friend, it had been the canned-meat company; doubtless with many more "clients" it had been the affair of the poisonous toys. Then, next time one of the Factsheets turned up . . .

"Neat," Grey said to the air. And added: "I want that man! What the hell is Casson playing at?"

For, though information was coming in almost daily, it still summed to nothing useful. Other people had been found who received the sheets, always anonymously, always in plain envelopes and never with the same post-mark twice. They were clearly hand-picked. They included people who handled the investment programme for unit trusts and some of the biggest insurance companies, the flywheels of the stock market, but not only such—also there were key men in the distribution chain of consumer products, like the head buyers for multiple stores, procurement directors for car accessory dealers and service-stations, the chairmen of export agencies handling millions of pounds' worth of British goods every year.

Every client named to him, Grey established, was in close enough contact with the financial world to learn quickly about the accuracy of the warnings which appeared in the shabby little leaflets.

Watching the course of the companies listed in the sheet Casson had given him, Grey detected the shadow of what had happened to Lupton & White in the gradual decline of Grand International Tobacco over the next few weeks, in the reversion of a former slow rise in another company, in the sudden cancellation of a takeover bid for yet a third.

On the spur of the moment he called Casson direct, and learned little enough for his pains. The envelopes in which the Factsheets arrived were the largest-selling brand in the country; the paper they were printed on was made by the largest mills; the typewriter was a discontinued model and could be one of several thousand still in use. Listening to the flow of excuses, Grey grew

abruptly angry. His vision of the publisher as a man
dealing in abstracts, manipulating the price of shares with
a kind of detached amusement in order to multiply his
own fortune, had grown concrete, and he was half en-
visaging them as team-mates, co-workers in double har-
ness.

"You have one more week!" he rapped. "If I'm not on
the mailing list for Factsheet Six I've finished with you
—is that clear?"

There was a moment of silence. Eventually Casson
cleared his throat.

"Well, there is one thing more it occurred to me you
could do," he said. "I hesitate to suggest it, but . . ."

"What is it?"

"You could advertise. Say in the *Financial Times*. I'm
certain the—ah—the publisher must read the financial
press very closely."

Grey was on the point of dismissing that as a ridiculous
idea, when he cancelled the words and reconsidered. In
sober fact, the points Casson had mentioned, like the
commonness of the materials used to prepare the Factsheets, did imply that it would be hard to breach the
wall of anonymity surrounding the publisher. And he did
want to find that man. He wanted it so much it was be-
coming an obsession. He kept finding himself daydream-
ing of the ways in which he could exploit the reputation
the Factsheets now enjoyed to drag down the price of
companies and let him buy into them, reorganise them,
and put them back on the market under new names
sponsored by what he referred to as his "magic."

But he was too impatient merely to copy the idea and
start his own monthly bulletin along similar lines. He
wanted the fund of goodwill—or rather, gullibility—which
the existing version had established.

Casson said, "I thought we should put a few anonymous
advertisements in other places, too, like—"

"Anonymous?" Grey cut in. "Christ, no! Are you out to undermine the good impression made by your occasional fits of insight? Why anonymous? If it's known that Mervyn Grey is interested in the Factsheet, this is going to give the guy the kind of cachet he's after, isn't it? It'll probably drive the last of the sceptics into his net. He'd love me for that! Yes, go ahead and place those ads at once—with my name on!"

Six days later the morning mail included a note typed on half a sheet of plain white paper, in an ordinary airmail envelope addressed to "Mr. Mervyn Grey, Mervyn Grey Enterprises, Grand Bahama Island." It ran, curtly enough:

I perceive you are interested in the forthcoming issue of my Factsheet. Well you might be. I shall be pleased to show you a copy personally. If you call, however, do so by yourself.

At the top there was an address, in a small town several miles north of London. At the bottom there was a name—George Handling. And not only was the typeface the same as that of the Factsheet, but so was the clumsy use of the machine, with a good half-dozen errors in the few lines of the note.

Jubilantly Grey told his secretary to book him on a flight to England as soon as possible. He was about to instruct her to put a call through to Casson as well, when he changed his mind. Even though the man's idea of advertising for the Factsheet's publisher had paid dividends, it had taken an unconscionable time for him to hit on it. Casson, he decided, was due to be discarded in favour of somebody younger and more enterprising, and it would be better to provoke him into resigning than to dismiss him openly. Best of all, of course, would be "retirement," not to salve Casson's feelings, because he regarded people who couldn't protect themselves as a liability and would not go out of his way to help them, but simply because it would do an inescapable minimum of damage to the image of his financial empire if the outside world were allowed to detect an internal disagreement.

So let it work this way, he decided: he would go to England without telling anyone he was coming, he would make his way to the home, or office, or whatever it was, of this Mr. Handling, and he would make him a proposition—a very good one. He might even offer him Casson's position, in due time, if his other talents matched his skill in exploiting credulity. It was going to take a person of fantastic ingenuity to make the most of the new vistas control over the Factsheet was opening up.

There had to be lavish tips, of course: to the airline staff, to ensure no one mentioned his arrival to the gossip columnists—almost every time he went to England he found a couple of journalists waiting for him—then, on arrival, to the ground staff at the airport so that he did not have to appear publicly among the passengers in the customs hall, and still later to the car-hire firm from whom he rented a small inconspicuous family saloon. He was, however, reasonably content with his precautions when he picked his way around the northern fringes of London under a dull autumnal sky which occasionally shed a half-hearted drizzle of rain. Tomorrow, or the next day, when Casson called with the latest of his useless scraps of information, it would be a real pleasure to announce that he had already been to see the man who published the Factsheets and closed a favourable deal with him. That would be the first of a series of carefully chosen wounds intended to compel Casson's eventual resignation. Then he could magnanimously offer retirement instead. It would work. He had done it often enough before.

Despite the gloominess of the afternoon he began to whistle as he drove along.

On reaching the small town which was his destination,

however, he grew puzzled. He had expected to find the street named on the letter he carried at the centre of the town; in his experience, even though businessmen decentralised away from the metropolis, they liked to centralise in the places they moved to. After much aimless driving back and forth, he asked a pedestrian and was directed to the outskirts, to a drab postwar housing development lacking all character and all charm. At the end of a cul-de-sac he found a large bungalow with one window lighted behind tight-drawn curtains, the garden before it overgrown with weeds, the door of the adjacent garage wide open to reveal that there was no car inside.

But the street bore the right name, and the right number was on the gatepost.

Grey parked the car and got out slowly. This low-income neighbourhood, this badly maintained house with its wild garden, did not fit his preconceived idea of the brilliant inventor of the Factsheets. Could he have been hoaxed? He reminded himself that the letter he had received was clearly from the same typewriter as the Factsheets, shrugged, and walked up the path, noticing that it was concreted where those on either side were spread with gravel and that the weeds had been cut along its edges despite the otherwise universal neglect.

It was full dark by now, and the nearest streetlamp was too far away to illuminate the front door of the bungalow. He went the last few yards cautiously, not wanting to trip over a step. There was no step. That struck him as peculiar, but he couldn't decide why. It was probably not significant, anyway.

He felt across the door-jamb until he located a bell, and pushed. Shortly an overhead light went on, and the door was opened for him.

"Yes?" a voice said, and then, changing instantly to a tone whose purport he could not decipher: "Ah, it's Mr.

Mervyn Grey, isn't it? Come in, please. It's cold and nasty out, I imagine."

Staring, he failed to respond for a moment. He hated to be at a loss, but this—this creature who had appeared before him was so totally askew from the mental pictures he had conjured up that he was astounded.

He was in a wheelchair, to begin with—a battery-operated wheelchair with controls on the right arm-rest. His left arm was shrivelled and the hand twisted, doubled back almost at right angles to the wrist. His legs were concealed under a grey blanket spotted with gravy marks and a smear of egg-yolk. Above a woollen shirt with a button missing, half his face was covered with an untidy brown beard, but the other half was a smooth keloid, almost purple, reaching from cheekbone to jaw. Both the eyes, however, were alert and piercing, and under their intent gaze he grew uncomfortable.

"Are you George Handling?" he forced out.

"That's right." The man in the wheelchair gave a nod.

"The person who publishes the Factsheets?"

"Yes! Look, don't just stand there—you'll make the house cold. I hate to keep the door open. Heating is bloody expensive these days."

But I should have thought you made enough from using the Factsheets to . . .

Grey bit the words back. Numbed by the possibility that all his deductions had been false, and he had merely stumbled across a lunatic after all, he stepped inside, and now had a chance to survey his surroundings. This was the oddest house he had ever been in. The reason for not having a step at the front door had been instantly clear when Handling appeared in his chair, but the logic of that went all through his home. The internal walls had been knocked away to give an open plan complete except for what he guessed must be a bathroom at the back. There was a bed in one place, with a curtain which could be drawn around it; there were cases of books in another, a desk with a typewriter on it in another, a lithographic press in another, stacks of paper and big cartons of envelopes nearby.

Moving with the automatic jerkiness of a puppet, he followed Handling across the floor towards the desk. There was a large paraffin stove burning there, of the convector-radiant type with a hot wire mesh glowing in the middle of a chromed reflector, but despite that and despite what Handling had said about shutting the door to keep the place warm the house was very cold.

Or was the feeling subjective, due to shock?

"Sit down," Handling said, swinging his chair expertly around so that it cleared the stove by inches. He tilted his head towards a chair with papers and a tea-cup on it. "Sorry you have to move all those things, but I can't dump them on the floor—they get in my way, for one thing, and I can't reach to pick them up, for another. I have to go and get my tongs if I drop something . . . Well! I suppose I ought to offer you a drink, oughtn't I? Only I haven't any. One doesn't get much pleasure out of it in my condition. I could make you a pot of tea, if you like."

Grey had found a spot for the cup and papers on the end of the desk, and taken a little longer than necessary in arranging them there, just in case there was a sample entry from the next Factsheet to be seen. But there was nothing of interest—only a stack of blank paper and half a dozen handwritten letters, upside-down.

"No—ah—no thank you," he said, forcing himself towards normality. "I suppose I should really have let you know when to expect me, but . . . Well, to be frank, your Factsheets have impressed me so much that the moment I knew where to find you I just dropped everything."

"Oh, there was no need to warn me of your arrival," the cripple said, and chuckled. "No need at all. I could

say I'm flattered at your taking the trouble to fly the
Atlantic just to call on me, but I doubt if there's any
need for that, either."

Grey's eyes roved the monstrous room into which the
house had been converted, spotting here and there among
the general bachelor disarray of shirts hung on chair
backs and stacks of old newspapers, items which gave
some anchor of credence to Handling's identity. He recognised the familiar red cover of the *British Industrial
Annual*, a number of commercial directories, publicity
material and prospectuses from various large companies
of which he himself had copies in his office on Grand
Bahama. He said, almost at random and to cover this
inquisitiveness, "Well, you'll have gathered from our advertisements that I'm most interested in your publication."

"Advertisements?" Handling said.

Grey blinked at him, and immediately had to look
away again—the sight of that fungoid patch of scar tissue
among the unkempt beard threatened to turn his stomach.

"Why, of course. That was why you wrote to me,
wasn't it? We advertised in the *Financial Times*, and
The Economist, and . . ." The words tailed away, and
he stared around again. Nowhere was there a sign, among
all the heaps of old newspapers, of the conspicuous pink
of the *Financial Times*.

"Oh, I wouldn't know about that," Handling said,
with a ridiculous attempt at a shrug which struck Grey
as rather horrible.

"Then how did you know I was interested in your
work?"

"It's a trade secret, Mr. Grey," Handling said, and
uttered a noise closer to a simper than a chuckle. "You've
seen at least one of my productions, haven't you? Then
you know I have a great many trade secrets."

Grey was conducting a furious debate with himself. An unclean cripple in a wheelchair was so far from the image he had mentally created of a gifted and prosperous market manipulator that he was half minded to dismiss Handling as the crank he had at first assumed when Casson showed him Factsheet Five. Yet there was incontestably a fund of credulity, tapped by Handling, which he could exploit if he got the chance. He would have to be tactful. Even if the man proved to have been deranged by his awful condition, he could be used.

"Yes, they impressed me enormously," he said, forcing warmth into his voice. He linked his fingers together, realised he had forgotten to take off his driving gloves, and decided against removing them now, because the house still felt bitterly cold. "Inside information like yours could be worth a fortune, handled in the proper way. In fact— Well, never mind that."

"You were probably going to say you're surprised to find the possessor of it living in a jerry-built bungalow in an ugly development on the fringe of a dull little provincial town," Handling said. His tone was quite unemotional. "But it's easier to keep out of people's way here, Mr. Grey. Besides, I no longer have any use for a fortune. I had a wife. I had a son. They both died in the accident which reduced me to this state."

"I—I'm sorry," Grey said inanely.

"Thank you for being sorry."

There didn't seem to be any way to follow up that remark. Casting about for a way to change the subject, Grey said, "But you must have some purpose in publishing these bulletins of yours. Or is it just a hobby?"

"It's more than just a hobby. It's practically a fulltime occupation. Compiling the information is a slow job in itself, and then there's the business of typing it up— I don't type either very fast or very well, as you can imagine—and making the litho plate and running off

the actual sheets, and addressing all the envelopes . . .
Oh, it keeps me very well occupied."

"I see." Grey licked his lips. "How do you manage to
have the sheets sent from so many different places? Do
you mail them yourself?"

"Oh, no. I seldom go further than the corner shop these
days, and if the weather's bad I try not to have to go
even that far. There's a commercial service which col-
lects them and takes them anywhere I choose within a
hundred miles for quite a small fee. I thought I'd muddle
the trail a little until I was ready to show myself."

That's something that bastard Casson missed! Thinking how his search could have been cut short by tracing
that mailing company, Grey said, "You have a big mailing list, do you?"

"I started with five hundred, picked more or less at
random," Handling said. "This month it will be over a
thousand."

"No wonder it keeps you busy! Ah . . . I'd have ap-
preciated being included in the list myself, by the way."

"Oh, you aren't at all the sort of person I aimed it at,"
Handling exclaimed. "I worked it all out very carefully.
When I say I started the list at random, I don't mean I
didn't choose the *kind* of person I wanted to receive
the Factsheet; all I mean is that I had no idea who was
likely to react. But there are certain key figures in the
financial world of this country, and you can find out who
they are if you put lots of little bits of information together—which is the sort of thing I'm used to. It took
me several months to make my list up, but that was all
right. I had plenty of time on my hands. Or rather, on
my *hand*." He picked up the limp left one with the live
right and regarded it curiously, as though he had come
upon a dead frog. "I selected people administering the
very big investment funds, people concerned with major
exports, people responsible for choosing the brands of

goods which are sold in the biggest chain stores all over
the country, and so on. People whose decision to accept
or not to accept a company's products could make or
break the company, do you see?"

Grey gave a cautious nod. "And why did you choose
them in particular?" he ventured. "I mean, in preference
to people like myself."

"Oh, because of the kind of information I was getting,"
Handling said. "They seemed to be the people who ought
to be told what I knew. You have seen the stuff I get?
You know what it's like?"

"Yes, of course I have. But why *that* information? How
do you come by it?"

"I'm a psychometrist. Psychometry is a branch of clair-
voyance. Actually I think the whole thing is simply part
of an all-embracing talent which will eventually be fully
revealed to us, but that's by the way. I get odd extras now and then—the curtain lifts, as the saying goes.
Sometimes I can analyse character, sometimes I can de-
duce or sense what a person is thinking, but my speciality
is being able to work out from objects their associations
with injury and death."

What a farrago of nonsense! All Grey's enthusiasm for
getting hold of the Factsheet mailing list evaporated on
the instant. He rose to his feet.

"Well, thank you very much, Mr. Handling. I'm sorry
to have taken up your time. However, if you're restrict-
ing your mailing list to—"

"Oh, really, Mr. Grey!" Handling cut in. "You didn't
honestly come all the way from the Bahamas for five
minutes' chat and not even a peek at Factsheet Six, did
you?" He added after a fractional pause, "This one is
devoted to firms you'd be especially interested in. You
were surprised that I hadn't seen your advertisements,
weren't you? But if you recall the letter I sent, it did say
that I had *perceived* your interest in my little venture."

Grey wavered. On the one hand, the cripple was certainly a crank, on the other, he had equally certainly influenced the market, so . . .

"Yes, I should like to look at number six," he admitted.

"I thought so!" Handling crowed, and moved his wheelchair around the desk, once more missing the paraffin stove by a fraction. He tugged open a drawer and peered in.

"Unfortunately it looks as though I only have spoiled copies left," he went on. "Yes, that's a spoiled one, and that's blank on one side, and— Never mind, it won't take a moment to put the second side on it. I still have the plate on the machine."

Dexterously he headed for the litho press. His deftness with only one hand, Grey conceded silently, was admirable, although everything he had to do was necessarily slow. He waited impatiently; meanwhile Handling, disinclined to hurry, chatted away.

"Yes, this talent of mine must I suppose always have been with me, at least in rudimentary form. For example, I never wanted to buy that washing machine which chopped my little boy's hand off, but of course it was a lot cheaper than all the others and we weren't exactly rolling in money, so I gave in. And I had my doubts about the sewing machine, too, but Meg couldn't go out to work for a long while after the—"

"Did you say your son lost his hand?" Grey interrupted in a dead voice.

"Why, yes. The washing machine wasn't fitted with one of these automatic brakes, you see, so you could have the what's-it going round while the lid was open, and without water in it spun amazingly fast, and poor little Bobby managed to turn it on and lift the lid, and . . . Ah, here we go now, or rather in a moment when the thing's warmed up. Yes, like I was saying, Meg couldn't go out to work for a long while after the sole-

plate of her iron fell on her thigh and the burn turned
septic—not much of an iron, but it was very cheap, of
course—and then this sewing machine she'd bought to
make a little extra at home ran wild and stitched across
the palm of her hand, and it was while I was driving
her to the hospital that it happened. The tyres on the car,
you see. I had my doubts about those as well, but we
were pretty skint, what with Meg not going out to work,
so I had to settle for what I could afford when it was
absolutely essential to fit new tyres, and there was Meg
crying and nursing her hand, and Bobby on the back
seat squalling because he didn't have a hand to nurse
any more, you see, and . . . Fine, here's your copy now.
Complete. Both sides legible."

He rolled back across the floor to a spot directly facing
Grey and held out the piece of paper, boldly headed
FACTSHEET SIX.

Mechanically Grey took it, but didn't look down. His
eyes were riveted on Handling's face. He heard himself
say, "So—what happened?"

"You mean, what caused the accident? Oh! Well,
according to the policeman who explained at the in-
quest, those tyres tend to spring away from the wheel
rim when you go round a corner fast—they're tubeless,
you understand—and of course this lets all the air out and
the car just goes completely out of control. In our case
we smashed into a lamp-post. Meg and Bobby were
lucky, I suppose. Certainly I couldn't have done much to
support them in this condition. As for me, I was in hospital four months.

"And it was while I was there that I began to discover
my talent. All of a sudden one day when I was being
given an injection I said, 'The last man who had a shot
from that syringe died, didn't he?' And they thought I
was just being morbid, but I felt sure. So I started following it up. And what I found was that I could—well—

sense when I took hold of something whether it, or anything like it, was going to hurt someone.

"At first I could only get snatches, but I had lots of
time, especially before I got this chair and had to wait
in bed for the nurse to call and attend to me. The
worst snag was that originally I thought the things I was
detecting had already happened, so I was sort of straining the wrong way into time to get at them. I can't make
it very clear, I'm afraid. I don't suppose it's happened
to many other people.

"Then I suddenly realised that I ought to be feeling
forwards, not backwards, and I got the proper hand of it.
Mark you, it could never be a quick job, working out
one of these things. Sometimes, especially with the real
mass-production items, I spent up to thirty-six hours
struggling before I sorted out what it was I was after and
could afford to go to sleep and rest up. So many options
were open, you see."

Almost hypnotised by Handling's burning intensity,
Grey still could not drag his eyes away from the ruined
face. He said, "But what exactly is it that you do?" And
reflected with paradoxical detachment that it made a
change for him to be dominated, however briefly. He
told himself he was putting up with it, though, because
he wanted to be completely convinced that the man was
out of his mind. Otherwise he might suffer pangs of disappointment at the failure of his dream about the Factsheet.

"It's more sort of what I did," Handling explained in a
thoughtful tone. "I told you—when I first started sensing
that the other things which matched what I was holding
would hurt such-and-such a number of people I thought
this was what had already taken place. But I found out
that sometimes the thing I picked on was too new to have
done all that, so then I realised the truth. I could sense
what was *going* to happen. Oh, no doubt you'll say, how

could I be sure? Well, I couldn't, could I? Not until I'd checked up. So I noted down everything I thought was exact, and whenever I got the chance I cross-referenced my notes. Like the Consumers' Association tests were very helpful, when they said that something I'd worked on was potentially harmful because it could give you an electric shock or whatever, and pretty often I found bits in the paper about food poisoning or toys that were dangerous to children and so on. After about a year or so, I was absolutely certain I was right."

"Oh, but this is ridiculous!" Grey forced out. "How could you know about—well, twenty thousand unwanted children, to take a really far-fetched example?"

"Well, that's harm, isn't it?" Handling said. "I mean, what can you do worse to a kid than let it be born when its parents don't want it? Every baby ought to be wanted!"

"Yes—yes! But the numbers, the *numbers!*"

"Oh! Sorry, I misunderstood you. Well, they sort of add up in my subconscious. I lie awake at night and I can feel them ticking away in my head. When they stop, I can feel how long they'll take to reach that total—three months, six months, a year. And then I write it all down. When the time is up, I put it into the current Factsheet and off it goes to all these people. I did think of other ways of spreading the news, but I decided they wouldn't work so well. I mean, the newspapers are dependent on their advertisers, aren't they? And the consumer journals have their own tests and their own way of going about it. Not as good as mine, but there it is. And people are definitely taking notice now. Especially since—you did say, didn't you, that you'd advertised to get in touch with me?"

"Yes." Grey bit the word off short, like the snap of wire-cutters.

"You could tell it was you, from the advertisements?"

"Yes!" Grey felt the prickle of sweat inside his clothes. How could he have imagined that this house was cold, and kept on his coat, his gloves, his scarf? It was boiling in here!

"Well, that certainly ought to convince everyone that I'm worth paying attention to," Handling said smugly. The virtual echo of his own remark to Casson galled Grey.

"It's a load of bunkum!" he exclaimed. "Taking hold of something or other and saying that during the next year it's going to hurt or kill so many people—you must be insane! And this Factsheet of yours is nothing more than a grandiose confidence trick!"

"You may not believe me, Mr. Grey," Handling said softly. "But the best part of a thousand people are going to, when they open their mail tomorrow morning. The mailing company collected Factsheet Six this afternoon, and it's on its way. Aren't you even curious to know what's in it this time?"

Grey raised the hand which held the copy he'd been given, intending to ball it up and march out, but from the corner of his eye he spotted three words that petrified him: *Mervyn Grey Enterprises.* Appalled, he read down the page.

Miracle Whirl washing machines electrocuted so many people through faulty wiring, started so many domestic fires, leaked and flooded so many homes, bringing down the ceilings on the floor below; Ee-Zee-Smoothe irons started so many other fires, came apart in use and burned the user, overheated and ruined so many expensive new garments; cars shod with Ultrac tyres were involved in so many fatal accidents, so many personal-injury accidents, so many damage-only accidents . . .

His head was ringing as he thought of the people to whom this list of accusations was going, and the buying power they controlled, and the markets they could slam the door on. He barely heard Handling say, "Yes, it was a Miracle Whirl which cost my boy his hand, and one of your irons that kept Meg at home so she had to try and make money sewing with one of your machines which stabbed her hand and it was Ultrac tyres I had to buy and which wrecked the car while I was rushing her to hospital. You have more than just blood on your hands, Mr. Grey. You have all kinds of suffering. You seem to have hurt at least one person for every day of your life."

"You bastard," Grey whispered. He thrust the leaflet into the side pocket of his overcoat. "I'm keeping this for evidence! It's libel—it's a filthy dirty stinking libel!"

"There's no libel about saying that a product is faulty," Handling said, and grinned. The effect was ghastly; only the bearded side of his face moved. "Oh, you could certainly sue me. I suppose I have committed a civil tort. But I haven't committed any kind of crime."

"You smug devil!" Grey roared, and hurled himself bodily forward. Cripple or no cripple, he *had* to wipe that grin off Handling's face!

But the impact drove the wheelchair backward, and it rammed straight into the paraffin stove—and knocked it over—and spilled a sea of blazing oil instantly over thirty square feet of the floor. Flames soared up, high as Handling's head. There was a sudden image seared into Grey's retinas, a distorted face with eyes perfectly round, mouth open in a choking gasp that drew in sterile oxygenless air, beard crisping and hair writhing like Medusa's snakes—

—and he was out of the house and the door was shut behind him and he was running for his car. He jumped in, started the engine, accelerated wildly down the road. Just before he turned out of sight, he glanced back. As yet, there was no sign of fire from outside the house; the curtains were drawn against the cold autumn night, and so were everyone else's on the street. That fact too became a still image in memory, like a stopped movie.

Forty miles away, on a lonely roadside, he braked the car again. Shivering, yet beginning to recover his self-possession, he forced himself to examine his situation rationally. It wasn't so bad—was it now? He could hardly conceal the fact of being in England altogether, but there was no reason at all for it to be known that he'd visited Handling's home town. He'd spoken to exactly one person, to ask directions—but he'd done so at dusk, from the shadowy interior of a car identical to thousands of others. Long before anyone realised that Handling's home was burning, he had been well clear of the town, perhaps over the county border. He concentrated on the memory of the deserted street. Yes, it could have been a long time before anyone noticed the fire.

And no one had seen him arrive, or leave, and that minor miracle of not taking off his gloves meant he could have left no fingerprints. And, above all, what was more likely than that a cripple should knock over his oil stove in a moment of inattention?

So he could drive quietly back to London, to the apartment which was always ready for him to walk into without notice, and he could go out nonchalantly to a club where he was known and have dinner and watch a good cabaret, and tomorrow morning about ten o'clock he could let it be discreetly known in circles where it counted that this time the Factsheet was a tissue of lies and the financial empire of Mervyn Grey Enterprise was in no danger, no danger at all, and—

The Factsheet!

Frantically he fumbled in the pocket of his coat and drew out the bit of paper. This was the only thing to link him with Handling. He must get rid of it at once. On the point of winding down the window and throwing it out, he cancelled the movement and instead took out his lighter. In another minute this could be anonymous wind-blown ashes and he would be safe. Oh, but there was the letter from Handling, of course! Lord! He had it with him, but had anyone seen it in the Grand Bahama office? Must have done! Well, then: just for insurance, he must walk into Casson's office in the morning, saying he'd been too tired to go straight there this afternoon, but he did intend to visit Handling and wanted Casson to come with him . . . Yes, that way would be all right, too. He'd be perfectly safe. Even if people believed the Factsheet and he lost a lot of money, he still had the talent which had made him the Boy Wonder of the Business World. He could survive.

Snapping the lighter, he held the copy of Factsheet Six towards its flame. The instant before igniting it, he stopped dead. This time, he was looking at the second side of the sheet. He was looking at a paragraph bordered with black lines, inaccurately hand-drawn with a wide felt pen.

Inside the border, in Handling's usual bad typing, it said:

This is the last issue of Factsheet. The publisher, Mr. George Handling of 29 Wyebird Close, Blentham, was murdered yesterday by Mr. Mervyn Grey in an attempt to stop this information being circulated.

He sat there for a long time thinking of a thousand people of great influence opening the plain envelopes which would arrive in tomorrow morning's mail. When he had finished thinking about it, he just sat.

FIFTH COMMANDMENT

"I'm not old," said Philip Grumman.

Outside, the waters of Lake Kannegawa sparkled in June sunshine, the ripples on its surface catching and breaking up the rays. Half a dozen pleasure-paddles and canoes drifted lazily on its waters, bearing some of the more energetic Retired on a journey to nowhere. Around the shore others lay dreamily sunning themselves.

"I'm *not old*," he said again, as though challenging Director Mackenzie to contradict him, and immediately changed his mind. "I'm sorry. Yes, I am sixty-eight, aren't I? So what you ought to say is, 'But I'm afraid you are old, Mr. Grumman.' Only you're too polite to do that."

Across the mellow top of his antique desk Mackenzie bestowed one of his invariable sleek smiles. He was an elegant man in his forties, which presumably made him the next-to-youngest person in the camp. The resident doctor, Masham, had a nurse to help him, but she was a plain and rather silent girl, not greatly liked.

"What you mean, Mr. Grumman," Mackenzie said now, "is that you're not senile. Well, who is nowadays?" He pointed through the wall-long window of his small and pleasantly decorated office towards where a group of men were playing leapfrog on the sand. "Are you perhaps worried about the risk of that eventually overtaking you?" he added. "If so, I can ask Dr. Masham to check you any time."

Grumman shook his head. He felt helpless, as though it wasn't worth spending breath on trying to make his point clear to Mackenzie. As Director of an Establishment for the Retired, his smooth composure was wasted. It could have weathered the stresses of a far more demanding job, and here it had practically nothing to resist. In general the Retired were a placid lot.

Sheep, thought Grumman, and wondered how long it had been since he actually saw one of those, or any domestic animal except a few dogs and cats. So many species had been wiped out by the war, not all during actual hostilities; many had expired afterwards, from mutated plagues or simply by being hunted so intensely for food that they became extinct.

But he'd seen sheep in a zoo once, years ago, and the metaphor survived.

How, though, could he break through to Mackenzie? He said abruptly, "Director, why are you here?"

"I'm afraid I don't quite understand," Mackenzie murmured.

You know perfectly well what I mean—

Grumman bit back his words with an effort, and thought: *It is true. Damn it. I am getting old. Age. Age and impatience go together. My mind is so deep in its traditional grooves it can't change course to contact other people.*

"What I'm getting at is this," he said. "You must have had a reason for choosing to come to Kannegawa. Why didn't you stay—uh—out in the world? I mean, nobody here except the medical staff is less than about twenty-five years older than you, and some of us are a lot more. So?"

"I see." Mackenzie nodded. "You're right. I thought long and hard about taking on this job. But I was told I'd be good at it—aptitude tests, you know—and I certainly find it suits me." He gave another smile, this time with a self-deprecating twist. "Perhaps I'm prematurely of Retired temperament myself. Perhaps I feel attracted to this quiet undemanding environment."

Grumman flashed his sharp grey eyes, like flint chips. He had no need for artificial aids to vision; he'd had proper training in self-correction.

"That," he said, "is so much nonsense and you know it."

And saw that at last he had succeeded in shaking Mackenzie's composure. The director was staring at him with unconcealed astonishment, the nearest to an unpremeditated reaction Grumman had ever seen from him.

"Why, nonsense?" he demanded.

"You're here because there are hardly any full-time jobs left on this planet. You wanted one of them, and all you could get was this. You're a busy man, Mackenzie, and because of that you're damned near unique!"

Mackenzie laughed, apparently with genuine amusement. He said, "You sound rather as though you envy me."

"Why shouldn't I?"

"Why should you?" Mackenzie's composure was back to normal. "After all, no one leads a better life than the Retired."

"An emptier life!" Grumman scoffed. He sat back in his chair, which was designed for extreme comfort, felt at a disadvantage in that relaxed posture and immediately sat upright again.

"Look, Mackenzie," he went on, "when you get Retired you'll have lived one of the few crowded lives there are left. You'll have the satisfaction of seeing the effort you invested pay off, even if only because you managed to keep this flock of sheep more or less contented. Can't you imagine what it was like for me, though, before Retire-

ment hit me? Hell, for sixty-eight years I've done *nothing!*
Nothing to look back on with pride, I mean. Until I was
twenty-one I was in school and college, getting an education. When I left, what did I do with what I knew? Jobs a
machine could have handled—would have, but that luckily someone realised before it was too late that men need
the illusion of work to keep them sane."

"You exaggerate," Mackenzie countered. "Your work
was genuinely worthwhile. You were in hydroponics,
weren't you? The world depended on people like you for
our mere survival. We'd have starved to death without
high-yield hydroponics."

"True, but all the groundwork had been laid long before I was born," Grumman argued. "Maybe when we
were clearing up after the war, and had to invent new
techniques to stay alive, maybe then—as you say—there
was a sense of achievement in my profession. I added
nothing to what I found when I took it up, and that's the
long and short of it."

Scowling, he thumped the front edge of Mackenzie's
desk, making an intercom phone rattle—an object which,
he had sometimes thought, was more of an ornament than
anything else, because inside the camp everyone always
knew where everyone else was and all the latest gossip
about what was going on.

"Then," he pursued, "three years ago I came here—to
what? Life imprisonment, that's what it amounts to!"

"Rubbish," Mackenzie said. "You came to a community
which is specifically designed to suit your needs and
those of the people around you. Instead of having to com-
pete with everybody else for services, having to compro-
mise, make allowances, adjust painfully to changes you
don't approve of, you find everything geared to your particular requirements."

"You make it sound like paradise," Grumman muttered.
"And I swear that isn't how it feels from the inside."

"Well, everyone bar you seems to disagree. I never heard any of the residents voice such a complaint before."

"Sheep! I keep telling you!"

"No, they are *not*," Mackenzie said, unexpected and indubitable warmth in his voice. "They are *people*. They are *human*. They do not behave in the least like any sort of animal, sheep or pig or monkey or anything other than people!"

Grumman, taken aback by his vehemence, was about to say something, but the director plunged on.

"Five hundred years ago, and come to that when we were rebuilding after the war, people did have to live like animals. Our ancestors slaved and starved and bowed their backs in manual labour. They'd done it since the dawn of history. And what had they to show for it? How proud do you think a broken-down old slave felt, looking at a useless monument like the Pyramids, testimony to the megalomania of a Pharaoh? We'd had a taste of what life could really be like before we were stupid enough to throw it all away in a crazy war, and after that we were determined never, never to go back to the old horrors. Those people yonder"—he gestured at the calm lake and the blue Canadian mountains beyond—"they're fulfilling their heritage of leisure. Their ancestors, and ours, devoted lifetimes to making possible Kannegawa, and Fildrey, and Piper's Green and all the others."

"Blasted fools," Grumman said, but there was little force in the words.

"Well, some people have claimed that they placed too much emphasis on leisure as an end in itself because they had scarcely any of it themselves. Fair enough; it may prove in the long run that we've gone to the opposite extreme. But as I told you, I've never had a complaint like yours before from any of the people who actually count, the Retired themselves, and the proof of the pudding . . ." A wave. "Who after all can tell what the purpose of humanity is, or even if it has one? As far as we know, perhaps as far as we shall ever know, the object of being human is—being human!" He gave a faint chuckle.

There was a silence. At length Grumman rose with a shrug and went out, shoulders bowed.

The corridor outside the office, like the office itself, had one wall completely of glass. Halting in sunlight Grumman muttered rebelliously, "I'm still in a cage, even if fifty generations are my jailers!"

The glass wall was as transparent as air. When he pressed his fingertips to it, though, they turned white. One of their by-the-book principles for making people happy was to bring the outdoors world inside to them, but nonetheless standing in this corridor he was physically enclosed. Glass could serve as well as iron bars to pen a man.

And he did feel shut in. He felt perpetually restless, on edge, and he didn't want to be doped with tranquillizers. He had the vaguest, faintest possible impression that he must not lose track of whatever was worrying him, but go on worrying at it until he dragged it into the open.

Maybe there was glass between him and it. Maybe he'd have to smash something first.

He wandered down the passage and along the gravelled roadway to the little chalet they had told him and Lorna to call home. But it wasn't home, and never could be. "Home" should be a place full of memories. The apartment he and his wife had occupied most of their married life had not been particularly smart, comfortable or spacious. Yet it was home. This chalet was no more than a box to store them in.

Of course, one thing had been missing from that apartment to make the concept of home complete. Much as he and Lorna had wanted children, they'd never had any, and consulting doctors had been fruitless. Over the years they'd grown accustomed to the fact, but it remained a permanent dull ache of frustration. A very common one.

Some of the weapons used in the war had induced recessive sterility, and their inquiries about adoption had been half-hearted because they knew there were almost no unwanted children nowadays.

Mackenzie had said that none of the other residents here had complained. Was that because everyone else had had the satisfaction of raising children? Possibly; one spoke little of outside matters here at Lake Kannegawa.

At the front gate of their little chalet, carefully designed to be different from its neighbours in shape, position on its plot, and name (no numbers: that too was a by-the-book principle), he paused to admire the flowers he had planted in the front garden, as he usually did on returning here.

Today, though, he saw nothing about them to admire. They were too neat, too tidy, as though attempting to imitate imitations. In a word, they looked artificial. Maybe he ought to grub them out and replace them with a good flourishing horde of wild growths. Wild growths . . . ? No, of course that wasn't the right term; it belonged to hydroponics, not to gardening. For a moment the correct word eluded him, and he felt a spasm of anger—yes, he *was* getting old! Then he had it, and spoke aloud: "Weeds!"

"Is that you, dear?" he heard Lorna call. Gruffly he answered, and continued around the house to find her stretched out on the back porch in the sun. From a few paces' distance he looked her over. She was still plumply attractive, although her sixty-four years had left inerasable lines on her face and neck, and several of those Retired who went in for spouse-swapping had invited her, and him, to join their revels. Long ago, though, when they would be forever childless, their interest in sex had waned, and they both found the idea not so much distasteful as tasteless.

She was better off in a way than he was, he reasoned. She still had her little make-believe worries about running the household, even though everything was made incredibly easy. There was still the pastime of "shopping"—not that one had to pay for anything, but there remained the fun of making individual selections. It was rumoured that a computer overrode the judgment of people who failed to choose items constituting a balanced diet; even so, the illusion was a comfort. Whereas he . . .

Shrugging, he bent to kiss her in the old familiar manner, and she smiled up at him. "Did you have a nice walk?" she inquired.

Sitting down beside her, he said, "I didn't take a walk after all. I went to see Mackenzie. Just on the spur of the moment."

"Oh, Philip!" Her tone was of mild rebuke; it had been long since either of them had been genuinely annoyed with the other. "You haven't been bothering him with your silly complaints, have you?"

"I chatted to him for a bit, that's all," he answered stiffly. "He told me a lot of things about Retirement which I suppose I hadn't clearly realised before. The history of it, and that kind of thing."

"That's good," Lorna said comfortably. "Don't I always say it helps to talk over your problems with someone else? But don't bother the director too much, will you? He's a busy man!"

Yes, you do always say that!

But Grumman was immediately ashamed for even thinking the words. This disquiet in his mind must reach horribly far down if it could disturb him even on that deep level where he still loved his wife as he had when he married her. Trying to blank his mind completely, he sat for a while in silence.

Then, without really intending to, he voiced a nagging question. His eyes wandering over the hedge separating their garden from that of their neighbours the Rockleys, he said, "Lorna, do Peter and Mary have any children?"

Startled, she blinked her eyes open, and a look of long-ago hurt turned down the corners of her mouth. At length she said, "No. I asked Mary once. She doesn't like to talk about it any more than we do, but she was glad when I told her we were in the same boat. In fact we wondered if that was why they made us neighbours."

She gave his hand a little squeeze and closed her eyes again, so that she failed to notice his reaction. A horrifying, absurd thought had crossed his mind.

The Grummans. No children.

The Rockleys. No children.

That man he'd been drinking with last week—what was his name? Ah, yes: Cassell. He'd been growing maudlin over his beer, because he was one of those pitiable men known as Retirement widowers; being more than five years younger than he was, his wife had exercised her option not to accompany him to Lake Kannegawa. And he'd said, explaining why his marriage had been a failure, that things would have been different if they'd had children.

But that wasn't all.

Surely, sooner or later in the past three years, one would have expected *somebody*—perhaps a stranger who didn't know him well, didn't realise it would be tactless —to bring out pictures, show off a letter, mention a locket containing a grandson's baby curls . . .

Even if he preferred not to think about children more than he could help, other people didn't feel the same.

Or did they?

All of them?

Everybody in the world?

He almost laughed at the absurdity of the notion. Hell, people at work had talked about their kids, hadn't they? And most times when they dropped around to see friends, there had been traces of the kids around, though usually they were away from home. There was this modern trend which he wasn't sure he approved of, this argument that you had to encourage independence from a very early age, so they went to schools run on self-governing lines, made their own decisions, even in vacation-time hardly came home except to sleep and not always then. If he'd had children presumably he'd have raised them the same way for fear they'd feel out of place and awkward, though it struck him as a waste to enjoy their company so seldom . . .

On the other hand, when they were brought by their teachers on conducted tours of the plant where he had worked, they'd seemed like such a damned nuisance! He chuckled at the recollection.

But the instantaneous nightmare had been terrifyingly vivid.

"Time for supper, dear," Lorna said eventually, when the sun was slanting towards the horizon. She rose and stretched contentedly. "And I thought we might go to the concert this evening. They're playing lots of our old favourites, you know."

"Fine by me," Grumman consented, and thought: *Our biggest problem in life is "what to do this evening." It's not enough. But what else is there that we'd be allowed to put in its place?*

He didn't know.

At the concert they found themselves by chance next to a genuine stranger, a new arrival from the outside world—the first in several months—who had come on his own because his wife, he explained, had been too tired after the strain of settling in. Lorna, excited, insisted on him coming to their chalet for coffee afterwards, and then when it grew late insisted equally vigorously on her husband showing him the way back, because as a long-time resident he would know the layout better, although in fact the camp was so simply arranged no one could possibly have missed his route. Grumman raised no objections; a late-night stroll, he reasoned, might help to settle his turbulent mind.

They went most of the short distance in silence. As they reached that stretch of the route which overlooked the night-calm lake, however, the new arrival—his name, Grumman had learned, was Stanley Wontner—halted, stared about him, and gave a deep sigh of contentment.

"Beautiful," he said. "So peaceful. I really am going to like this life."

Then you're one of the lucky ones, Grumman thought sourly, and recalled Mackenzie's comment about the proof of the pudding. The thin sharp starlight showed him a smile on Wontner's face. Without really intending to, he asked the question whose answer might perhaps confirm his own lingering suspicion that raising children would have given him the same sense of achievement in later life which this man obviously enjoyed.

"Say, Stanley! You and Mrs. Wontner have kids, I guess?"

The smile vanished from the other's face. He said in a tight voice, "No. Sadie and I always hoped, but . . . Well, I guess we just weren't among the lucky ones." He hesitated. "You?"

"Guess we weren't lucky either," Grumman said.

There was a pause. Eventually Wontner said, "Well, all this fresh air has made me sleepy. My chalet is right over there—I better make for it and turn in. As soon as we're settled, you two will come over, won't you?"

"Yes, of course," Grumman assured him, thinking: *Because we're companions in loneliness? He'll soon find out how few people here talk of children.*

He lay awake for hours that night, and overslept next morning in consequence. Lorna was worried by that, and he had to fend off her anxious inquiries all through his belated breakfast. Finally, to shut her up, he had to promise that he'd drop by at Dr. Masham's office for a checkup—the last thing he wanted to do, owing to that nagging notion he'd experienced for so long, the feeling that he must cling to his unformulated worry until it became clear. However, when he'd promised, he had to go.

There was no one else in the quiet, comfortably furnished waiting room of the surgery except the plain young nurse-receptionist, who recognised him, greeted him and informed the doctor via an intercom that Mr. Grumman was here. Masham's voice crackled back with instructions to come straight in.

He waved Grumman to the usual chair, tipped his own chair back and asked what the trouble was. As Grumman summed it up—a touch of insomnia, he called it—his mind worked busily. He liked Masham rather better than Mackenzie; most of the men seemed to, whereas the director's fireproof composure appealed more to the women residents, including Lorna. Perhaps a contributory factor was that Masham was nearer his own age, some ten years or so older than Mackenzie judging by appearances. For example, his hair was touched with grey, if only at the temples.

It would probably be easier to put his crucial question to Masham. If he got the chance.

The chance came easily. Having run a couple of simple tests, touching electrodes connected with his diagnostic desk to Grumman's scalp, chest and back, Masham gave a shrug and resumed his seat.

"Nothing physically amiss," he said. "Have you any idea yourself why you should be sleeping badly?"

"Yes," Grumman said, drawing a deep breath. "I've been wondering why nobody here has any children."

And waited.

"I see," Masham said finally, in a neutral tone.

"I'm right, then?" Grumman tensed. "Nobody here is a parent, not out of all these hundreds?"

Masham inclined his head gravely. "That's correct."

"But—"

"Mr. Grumman, haven't you ever wondered why Lake Kannegawa is such a small establishment? You said, 'all these hundreds of people'—and you're right: there are only hundreds of residents here. Seven hundred ninety-two at this morning's count, including Mr. and Mrs. Wontner, who arrived yesterday. Most Retirement centres are far, far bigger, aren't they? Fildrey, for instance, is a fair-sized town, with about twenty thousand people. But Lake Kannegawa serves a special purpose."

"It's for people without children?"

"Precisely. So that—well, so that salt isn't rubbed in the wound."

Grumman gave a slow nod, but said nothing. Masham went on solicitously, "Of course, if this environment disturbs you, arrangements could probably be made to transfer you to another centre . . . ?"

"Lorna seems to be perfectly happy here," Grumman muttered. "But I'll—I'll consider the idea. Thanks very much, Doctor. I'm sorry to have taken up your time."

"Not at all. That's what I'm here for. And just in case your insomnia recurs, I'll give you a prescription for some tranquillizers."

For the first time, as he left the surgery, Grumman felt his age as someone a thousand years before might have felt it: stiffening his joints, slowing his mind to a dull turgid pond, wearying him beyond description. Reaching a junction on the path, he paused and stared around, remembering how Wontner last night had said, "Beautiful!"

Yes. *But* . . .

He had intended to turn back towards the lake, where as always people were sunning, swimming, paddling their little toy boats around. Abruptly he realised he couldn't face company right now. It wasn't only the Rockleys, the

Cassells, the Wontners, the Grummans, who were deprived of children. It was everyone he was ever going to meet again until he died.

Except Mackenzie? Except Masham?

He shook his head. Doubtless they'd thought of that too, whoever *they* might be. Throughout his long career in hydroponics he had learned to trust the foresight of those who now made plans for the planet's future; often and often polite memoranda had drawn his attention to details he himself might have overlooked, so he knew how cautious and exact they must be. Admirably so, of course, given the tumultuous and catastrophic errors which marred the past . . .

No, it would create too dangerous a focus of jealousy to have staff in residence who weren't afflicted like their charges. One careless word might touch off a crisis.

So there must be another reason for Mackenzie having accepted his post here, besides those which he'd talked about yesterday.

Absently, preoccupied with the idea of transferring away from this special camp, he found his feet carrying him up a slope away from the lake. He went on grass, and shortly among shrubs that hid the lake-shore from sight. It was unexpectedly pleasant to be on his own like this, and he kept right on going until a sudden pang of hunger nudged him out of his brown study. His stomach was conditioned to the regular routine of the Establishment.

Glancing around, he was surprised to find how far he'd wandered, at least a couple of miles, clear to the foot of the ring of hills enclosing the lake. Ahead there was no path, just steep ground that grew increasingly rocky as it rose.

On the point of turning back, he checked and thought: *Why, this is the first time I've come so far since I arrived here! I've been acting as though Kannegawa is all there is. Maybe that's part of my trouble; maybe that's helping to make me feel old? But I'm not. I'm fit enough to scram-*

*ble up that hill, and it's lovely countryside all around
here, and the exercise might clear some of the cobwebs
from my brain.*

With determination he stepped away from the rough
path he had been following and headed directly up the
slope.

But he had gone only a few hundred yards, and risen
perhaps thirty-odd feet, when he grew puzzled at the
view ahead. Those hills: they looked somehow closer
than they ought to be. They looked bluer than they
should from this short range, as blue as they did back
by the lake-shore.

A vast nameless fear hovered at the back of his mind,
but he fought against it and strode onward.

Among the hills. Past them. They disappeared.

Kannegawa *was* all there was.

There were no mountains.

This was a different world.

He stood on the top of a slight rise. Before him there
was land under cultivation: ridges of brown earth separated by furrows, tidily spined with tall plants that he
recognised. Corn.

But you didn't grow corn in open ground—not since
the war!

Confused, beginning to be frightened, he glanced over
his shoulder. At his back there was nothing but mist—a
wall of silvery haze that stayed where it was despite the
tugging of a light breeze.

A humming noise startled him. He jerked his head
around again to find that a vehicle was skimming along
above the plants, like nothing he had ever seen. Not an
aircraft: a flat object like an oyster shell, travelling
smoothly on an invisible road of solid air. It was silent except that its passage left a wake of musical vibration, like
a giant trying to tune a violin.

Turning in astonishment to see where it was heading,
he caught sight of something on the horizon. A city? It

must be a city. But it was *tall!* To one side of it a vast tower rose, jutting perhaps three thousand feet into the sky.

Something glinted, very high in the air. Straining his still good vision to the utmost, he made out that it was growing larger. Descending.

It took on an oval shape, flattened at its base. It was vast beyond his conception of proper size, and it too was not an airplane. It *fell.*

He shouted aloud and covered his eyes in horror as the thing dropped like a stone towards the city. But the crash he expected did not come, and when he looked again it was standing upright beside the towers and was not dwarfed by them.

"We had hoped to spare you this," a soft voice said from behind him. He spun around. Mackenzie stood there, perhaps having emerged from the silvery mist—but how, without making a sound? There were pebbles underfoot. It didn't matter; here he was.

"That—that city!" Grumman forced out. "If it is a city—"

"Of a kind," Mackenzie agreed. His face was set in a thin sad smile, utterly different from the professionally ingratiating expressions Grumman had always seen him wear before.

"But I never heard of anything that looked like that!" The world was canting to a crazy angle around Grumman. "And this corn, growing right out in the open! I was in hydroponics—I'd have known if something like that was going on! All this can't have happened in two years!"

"It's taken two hundred," said Mackenzie.

Needing to steady himself, Grumman stumbled to a boulder a few paces distant and leaned back against it, his eyes drawn again as though by a magnet to the spectacle of those majestic towers. He said, "Oh my God. For pity's sake, explain!"

"If I do explain," Mackenzie warned, "it's unlikely that you'll be allowed to remember what I tell you."

"What?" That was too much for Grumman. He ignored the implications of the remark, and repeated, "Explain!"

"Just a moment," Mackenzie said, and seemed to listen to the wind for a while. At length he said, "Very well. I'm permitted to tell you what you want to know. There will be others here in a moment; we can talk until they arrive. Go ahead."

"Who are you?" Grumman demanded. "Or . . . No. *What* are you?"

"A man. What else? But"—Mackenzie hesitated—"not quite the same kind of man as you."

"I don't understand!" Grumman cried.

"I'll give you an example." Mackenzie bent to pick a pebble from the ground. He held it in the air before him, between finger and thumb, and then took his hand away. It did not fall.

"How . . . ?" But Grumman's voice failed him.

Mackenzie shrugged. "I can't say how, any more than you can say how—oh—how you digest your food. But basically you see only the reasons why things should fall. I can sense reasons why they should not."

In a hoarse whisper Grumman said, "How many of— of *us* are there left?"

"About three hundred thousand," Mackenzie said. His voice was kindly but his words were relentless. "All of them are now Retired."

"And none of them had children?"

"None at all."

"But how did you hide from us?"

"Did we have to? Until this moment, could you have guessed that I wasn't what you assumed me to be?" Mackenzie took hold of the floating pebble and tossed it aside. "Besides, we couldn't hide. We're everywhere.

"After the war, you know, there wasn't much left. But we kept the worst of the details from you. Do you realise that there were nearly four billion people on this planet when the war broke out? Right now there are barely fifty *million*. And almost all of us who are alive now have been —well—changed. We're not sure what triggered that off; it could have been radiation, but more likely it was a chemical mutagenic weapon which lingered indefinitely in the ground and water. Radiation is much too random to have caused such a widely spread genetic alteration. We—I'm sorry, but there is after all a difference!—we appeared simultaneously on three continents, and the odds against radiation causing that are incalculable.

"But never mind that. What counts is that we're talented in certain unprecedented ways, and above all we're a great deal more stable. You know that some of our earliest ancestors were out-and-out cannibals, preferring the meat of their own kind above anything else. We gave up that habit. In the same way, the habit of fighting has now been given up."

Pithecanthropus, homo pekinensis, Neanderthal man, all seemed to be looking out through Grumman's eyes, listening with his ears to the pronouncement of a sentence of doom. Grumman whispered, "But you did hide from us! How? *How?*"

"I see what you mean. Well, you made that easy. Even before the war there was a tendency for people to huddle into small closed private groups, disliking and even hating those outside. When, later, it became a matter of life or death to stay in the few safe uncontaminated places, we simply encouraged the habit. Thus we maintained your little world for you, which you'd already reduced to half a dozen cities—"

"And sent your children to look us over as though in a zoo!"

"Unkind," Mackenzie said. "Many of us live in those cities even now. You knew many of us, called us friends."

"The ones with children?"

"The ones with children," Mackenzie confirmed. "Who

were never at home when you called, for fear they—less disciplined than adults—might give the secret away."

"Did you make us sterile?"

"That work was done for us, I'm afraid." The pity of a million years coloured the soft voice. "Those weapons that attacked the gonads were so efficient, it took only six or seven generations for the recessives to link up in every survivor we know about."

"Then how can you—?"

"We make ourselves," Mackenzie said simply. "That's perhaps our greatest talent. We can cleanse, shape, overhaul the very molecules in our cells. This healthy, crop-growing land you see before you: we made it like that, wiping away the scars of nuclear attack, dispersing the poisons, restoring the humus, the soil-bacteria, the ground of life. It is very hard to make a viable human being now, but we can do it."

"And *we* can't."

"What you learned to do," Mackenzie said sternly, "was to unmake mankind."

"So you shut us up in jail, by way of punishment!" Grumman snapped.

"Jail?" Mackenzie said, and let the echo serve as its own comment. He went on: "Could you have endured a world where the mind has become a better tool than the hand? You resented the incursion of mere machines into the domain of work. You were cursed with a dream; you couldn't endure it when it came true. But we can. At least, so far we've found that we can."

"That—that egg-shaped thing over there," Grumman said, mastering himself with much effort. "Is it a spaceship?"

"Yes. Landed a moment ago from the moons of Jupiter. We mine the dense gases of the planet for valuable compounds. And we are planning to make a first trip to the stars."

"I wish I hadn't asked you to explain the truth," Grumman said greyly. "Before, I thought I was merely useless. Now I know I'm a parasite."

Mackenzie seemed about to reply, but there was an interruption. A tiny grinding of gravel caused Grumman to glance around, and there, almost within arm's length, was the plain nurse-receptionist who worked for Dr. Masham. She had come from nowhere. She had simply —arrived.

"Dr. Masham will be here in a moment with transport for Mr. Grumman," she said.

Yes. I can hardly go back on the route that these people use . . .

The thought was barely complete when one of the strange shell-shaped vessels fell from the sky with the same gravity-defying swoop as the ship from Jupiter. It stopped without rocking, inches above the ground, and Dr. Masham looked out from it with a sad smile like Mackenzie's. Saying nothing, he gestured an invitation for Grumman to step aboard.

"Don't worry," Mackenzie said. "You'll be freed from the memory of all this. It won't even remain to haunt your dreams."

Briefly Grumman was minded to refuse, but—well, what other course was there for him to take? He had been dumped on the junk-pile of history, and that was knowledge no one could live with and stay sane.

On the point of obeying, one foot already inside the little craft, he checked and turned back to Mackenzie.

"But why?" he said. "Why did you go to all this trouble, keeping up our let's-pretend world? Why didn't you simply—?"

"Get rid of you?" Mackenzie said in horror. "Our *parents?*"

Time seemed to halt for a heartbeat. Then, proudly, Grumman climbed into his sons' ship.

FAIRY TALE

The Pig and Whistle Inn,
Dartleby, Devonshire

To Professor Sir Leo Courtenay,
The Montague Laboratories,
Cambridge

Dear Leo,

This is not exactly a letter from the grave, although since you presumably gave me up for dead seven years ago as everybody else seems to have done, doubtless that will be your first reaction on seeing my handwriting. Yes, I *am* your old friend Barney Gregg, who disappeared down here on Dartmoor in the summer of 1964, and I propose to call on you and convince you of that fact as soon as I have calmed sufficiently from my present agitated state. Can you imagine the shock experienced by someone who went to sleep in 1964 and woke to find that it was 1971? I suspect not; that's what happened to me, as I am compelled to believe on seeing the newspapers, yet the sheer improbability of such an event creates a kind of obstinate blockage in the mind, and I cannot rid

myself of the notion that this is all some terrible nightmare . . .

Which, very definitely, it is not. I think you know me
well enough—but there I go again, forgetting that seven
years *have* gone by, seeming to me like a single night.
You knew me well enough, let me say, to recognise that
I was never a man to be easily deluded, or to let enthusiasm run away with him. Indeed, although I was (and
suspect that physically I still am) on the right side of
fifty, I was quite pleased to be referred to as "Old Sober-
sides." I regarded it almost as a professional compliment.
Should not a barrister be the most sober of men?

Please, therefore, suspend your judgment on the following remarkable narrative until you have perused it
in toto. I am going to set down facts—I repeat, *facts*—
which I have weighed in my own mind as carefully as I
would weigh the evidence of a witness in court. Though
they will strike you as extraordinary it is imperative that
you should not dismiss them out of hand.

I ought perhaps to explain why I am writing to you before contacting anyone else concerning my return to the
everyday world. I have spent much of this evening reading feverishly through what newspapers I could lay
hands on in this isolated village. By chance I saw in the
Times that you are now heading the Montague Laboratories, and I realised that as you are the only nuclear
physicist with whom I am on intimate terms I must communicate with you at once. (Congratulations on securing
your present post, by the way, and on your knighthood,
which comes as news to me although for all I can tell it
may have been conferred years ago.)

I did think of telephoning you, but I was forced to the
conclusion that a written message would be more effec-
tive because more studied and deliberate. I have been
"back" only since this morning, and I shall certainly be in
no fit state to travel for a while yet; moreover I haven't a

penny to my name and shan't have until my bankers react to the telegram I sent them—may they respond with
promptness!

Here I am, then, sitting up after midnight in a tiny
dusty room under the eaves of this pub, penning a story
which the old people in Dartleby find more credible
than do I to whom it happened. But then I suppose they
accept their legends as an integral element of history.
"There's piskies oop to Dartymoor," as the local folk have
been saying for generations.

First you will wish to know where I have been these
seven years. Well, my dear Leo, not to put too fine a point
on it, I have been *in Fairyland,* and there is a rational
basis for the stories told about Rip van Winkle, Thomas
the Rimer, and all those other fabulous characters.

Already I see you in my mind's eye, scientifically
scornful. For God's sake—and far more for Man's sake
—defer judgment. This is what took place.

Everyone in this village has turned out to be intimately
acquainted with the story of my disappearance. I seem
to have provided a lasting sensation, and I swear many of
them are disappointed at my return. Much may have in-
tervened to put the facts out of your mind, however. To
refresh your memory: I was on one of my annual camping trips. You, and most of my other friends, were never
able to understand why I preferred to spend my holidays
alone in a tent instead of in some hotel on the Riviera
rubbing shoulders with the *haut monde.* Frankly, my
legal practice exposed me to so much duplicity and chi-
canery that I needed to escape from my fellows at least
for a week or two every summer. (How curious to be con-
tinually forcing myself to use the past tense: as though
one were translating a Latin exercise and having to recall that it was the Roman custom to compose letters
from the recipient's point of view!)

The moors of the West Country have always been my favourite retreat—mainly, I think, because out here one can let one's imagination stretch its legs. Wishing-wells and ends of rainbows no longer seem as remote as they do in London. When the early mists swirl around the grey tors, there seems no reason why strangely garbed Phoenician traders should not appear and barter with us for tin. I mention this fanciful notion deliberately, to indicate that I fully appreciate I was in a susceptible state upon my arrival here.

The drive from London was a long one, and when I reached Dartleby the weather was bad—drizzling with rain and very windy. However, I was too impatient to postpone the commencement of my week's camping even to the following morning. I garaged my car here at the inn and walked westward with my tent and rucksack, stopping only to buy milk at a lonely farm.

On being overtaken by darkness, I pitched camp in the shelter of a group of high grey rocks, because there I found a kind of shallow cave where I could build a fire and sit in slightly greater comfort than inside my little tent. After eating a light supper—which, by the by, did not include any of the traditional ingredients for nightmare, not even cheese—I doused the fire and turned in, expecting to sleep as soundly as I generally do under canvas and awaken an hour or so after dawn.

However . . .

Now, as I had mentioned, I'd paused to buy milk from a farm I passed. I had the better part of a quart in an aluminium jug. Stupidly, I had omitted to bring its lid; accordingly, before I retired, I had set it on a flat stone near the tent and covered it with an enamel plate. For fear the wind might lift the plate off, I had weighted it with another large stone.

About midnight I was woken by a sharp clanging noise. I knew it instantly for the sound of the plate being dislodged. I assumed at first the wind had been responsible. Listening, however, I found that it had dropped and that it was no longer raining.

I crept cautiously to the door of the tent and looked outside. And I saw—

How best can I describe the creature? I could see it, or *him,* distinctly by the watery light of the moon, now the clouds had blown by. My first thought was of a lemur, or loris: a spindly limbed upright animal, no taller than the length of my arm, with huge eyes and prick ears like paper cones point downward on the sides of its head. This apparition was endeavouring to raise and drink from my jug of milk—a task which in proportion to his size was comparable with a man trying to drink from a gallon keg.

As I have confessed, on leaving London that morning I had unconsciously divested myself of my habitual city-dweller's scepticism, and I had not a moment's doubt that I was seeing one of the famous "Little Folk" in the flesh. A Dartmoor pisky, in fact.

I was so excited that I made an unintentional noise. At once the creature took fright. With a high squeak like a bat's—but obviously not so shrill, for I have not heard a bat cry since I was a lad of sixteen—he let the jug rock back where it stood and vanished among the boulders.

Eager to tempt him back, I poured some milk into the plate as one would for a cat, and made idiotic mewing noises into the darkness. Shortly I saw the little fellow again. He was so pathetically eager for the milk that eventually his desire overcame his fear of me and he dashed up to suck at it. He definitely sucked; he did not lap or drink. His tongue seemed to curl into a tube like a proboscis.

I could inspect him at leisure now. Although his limbs were not dissimilar from the human, his body was very different indeed. What at first glance might have been mistaken for a stubby tail coiled between his legs proved to be as it were his abdomen; it was separated from the point at which the limbs set into the trunk by a very narrow "waist." Despite being no biologist, I was at once struck by the insectile quality of such an anatomy, and suspected that in the course of evolution the thorax must have lengthened and the abdomen shrunk to permit an upright stance, while one pair of limbs atrophied or fused with its neighbours.

I had, of course, visions of taming the creature, or at least of luring him back for many more helpings of milk, as one can with a hedgehog. So I remained very still, watching him intently, and it was not long before I noticed how strangely he had begun to act. By the time he had half drained the plate his legs seemed to weaken, and he had much trouble keeping his balance. Once he fell over completely, and regained his feet only with difficulty, clutching mightily at the plate to steady himself while he resumed his sucking.

It occurred to me suddenly that he must be intoxicated!

He straightened abruptly and uttered another shrill cry. Then he began a sort of wild dance, arms and legs flailing. I was too astonished to react until he had cavorted away from me and was almost lost again among the rocks. Seizing my flashlight, I hurried after him, careless of the fact that I was barefooted.

Just inside the mouth of the cave where I had cooked my supper, I found him sprawled flat on his face, exactly like a dead drunk human being. He had tripped over an unburnt stick and tumbled into the damp, dirty ashes of my fire. (I almost blush to admit how I had extinguished it . . . but that, I may say, did not contribute to the salubriousness of the situation!)

Focusing my light on him, I bent to pick him out of the messy pile, and a falsetto voice like that of an incredibly precocious baby sternly ordered me not to touch him.

I was sufficiently taken aback to straighten to my full height—a dangerous thing to do in a low-ceilinged cave. I cracked my head so painfully that it was a minute or two before I saw clearly again. When I did recover, I found another of the creatures bending over his fallen companion, exactly like Toby Ritchie at the bedside of a patient in St. Helen's. (You know Toby, I think, in which case you will understand the comparison at once.)

It was this new arrival who had told me to leave the unfortunate drunkard alone. He spoke again a moment later, raising his head but averting his large round eyes from the glare of my flashlight. In a tone of distinct anger he said, "You gave him milk!"

"Well, actually I did," I admitted.

The creature sat back in the posture a man would call "squatting on his haunches," and I saw that this species could have no need of chairs, for he rested very conveniently on his padlike abdomen.

"You ought to be ashamed of yourself!" he snapped.

As calmly as possible I said, "I'm very sorry. I found him trying to help himself from my milk-jug. I thought I was doing him a favour."

He looked me over as well as he could, shading his eyes from my light. After a moment he moved, in a kind of frog's hop, to take station behind his companion. More doctorlike than ever, he leaned his full weight on the other's abdomen and pumped back and forth as though giving artificial respiration.

A few applications of pressure in this way caused the "patient" to regurgitate a stream of discoloured milk. I began to refer to the "doctor" in my own mind as Toby, for reasons indicated earlier.

"Better," said the newly baptised Toby at last, and heaved and dragged his companion into a more comfortable position clear of the wet ashes. "But I'd hoped we'd never suffer this again. Must we wait for ever to be free of it?"

Inspiration dawned. "Am I to understand," I ventured, "that milk is poisonous to you? A kind of dangerous drug?"

"Isn't it common knowledge?" he retorted.

"Not to me, I assure you! For us it's the most harmless of substances. I took it for granted your friend was simply thirsty."

"I'll take your word for it," the creature said after a pause. "It's true enough that things have changed since the days when every farmer's wife would set milk at the door to tempt us. Some of us became so debased by lust for milk that they would even curry favour by working on the farms, in spite of the continual danger from cold iron."

That put a different complexion on the old stories of the fairyfolk doing favours for humans who treated them well! And reminded me of an all-important question. I said, "So you are—uh—one of what we call the Little People?"

"See for yourself," he sighed, and gave a kind of shrug. From under a pair of brownish, shaggy, shawl-like cases on his back he shook out wings as gauzy as a beetle's. Somehow I never felt when I was a child that whimsical artists were correct in decorating fairies' backs with butterfly wings, and here in my sceptical middle age I'd been proved right.

"Can you fly?" I asked.

"Of course not," was the impatient answer. "They're vestigial."

It was his use of that relatively technical word which made me see what I ought to have realised when he so professionally relieved his companion of the poisonous bellyful of milk. This was no . . . How shall I put it? This was no *peasant*, if you like. Toby bore no resemblance to the traditional mischievous pisky of West Country folklore, and indeed if that image was founded upon what we would call a group of "hard drug addicts" the

fact was scarcely surprising! No, what I had to deal
with here was a true sapient being, with an exceptional
vocabulary and doubtless many other talents specific to
his kind. I was suddenly overawed at the notion that I
was speaking, as it were, to an alien intelligence. An ancient dream had turned to reality for me. I was desperate
to make the most of this unique encounter, yet at the
same time mortally afraid I might give unlooked-for offence through ignorance and cause him to vanish into the
night. Casting around for some way to indicate that I
was concerned about his well-being despite what other
members of my race might have done, I hit on something
he had hinted at.

"I think you said that iron is dangerous to you also," I
suggested. "There's probably iron in this flashlight of mine
—is that harmful?"

Seeming willing enough to talk, he shook his head. "It
isn't iron as such, or stainless steel. It's rust. It's an irritant.
Touching rusty iron sets up an allergic reaction. Without treatment the victim suffocates in a matter of hours."

"Suffocates?" I echoed.

"You have internal lungs. Ours communicate directly
with the air. So." Folding his wings, he twisted where he
sat to display the front of his chest—no, call it a thorax,
because this seemed like conclusive proof that Toby was
basically an insect. I recalled reading that insects larger
than a certain size could not survive because oxygen
could not percolate far enough into a system of rigid
spiracles such as they use for inhalation. Toby's species
solved that problem, he informed me, by making almost
the entire thorax into a pseudo-lung, convoluted until its
area was greater than that of the body-surface. Rust in-
flammation, I gathered, made this pseudo-lung imperme-
able and horny.

With equal willingness he demonstrated to me how it
was possible for him to talk, using a specialised vibratory

organ located close to a large air-cavity in his thorax that acted as a resonator. Fascinated, impressed, bewildered, but ultimately emboldened by his openness, I came finally to the crucial question.

"There's something I simply don't understand," I said. "Your race is plainly very intelligent, and the way you're talking to me indicates that you must be in close contact with us, to employ such a vast range of English words. Why have you become a half-forgotten legend to us?"

"Almost all of us have gone," he replied. "We had begun to leave when you were still wild beasts without a language."

"Gone? Do you mean—died out?"

"No. Gone. Departed. To other worlds or other modes of existence. You have no adequate words. Perhaps if you last two or three thousand more years . . . Until a century ago, you know, it was barely possible for us to communicate with human beings, and even now I find it difficult to pare down my thinking so that I can express myself within the confines of a human tongue."

"Then you must be an older race than we are?"

"Considerably," he agreed, not without a trace of dry humour. "Our best estimates indicate that we have—ah—*been around* for between thirty and sixty million years."

Million! The shock of that almost drove out of my mind the next thing I had intended to ask, but I forced myself to recover; I must not waste a second of this unrepeatable opportunity. I said, "I'm afraid my light is rather bright for you, isn't it? Are you purely nocturnal?"

"Primarily," was the reply. "And if you would turn the beam aside . . . ? Thank you. Yes, our eyes are adapted to low light-levels, but that's a secondary characteristic. Our ancestors possessed a chitinous integument which, as you've seen, has evolved into no more than a sort of skeleton to anchor our muscles, a process not dissimilar from that which generated the sea creatures you call squids from the original type of the Mollusca. Consequently in warm dry air we dehydrate very rapidly. Also we are sensitive to ultraviolet light; there is a risk of a condition akin to lupus, or cancer of the skin."

"Can you not wear protective clothing?"

"We prefer not to. It would hamper our breathing and the continual exchange of moisture which occurs everywhere on the surface of our bodies. In any case, the sun can easily be avoided in moist temperate areas like this island."

There were still hundreds of things I wanted to know, particularly about how closely our legends resembled fact, and above all I meant to inquire how his race—so fragile that sunlight or a bit of rust could kill them—had endured these millions of years, whereas we tough humans seemed in imminent danger of exterminating ourselves after a mere fraction of that time.

At the same moment, however, his sick companion stirred and sat up, and I realised that Toby had only been talking to me to occupy my attention until the latter recovered. He turned, and my bruised scalp started to tingle. It was plain that there was a conversation in progress, but it was in the ultrasonic range.

At length, looking thoroughly ashamed of himself, the toper made off, and Toby addressed me again.

"This has been interesting," he said in a friendly enough manner. "Almost certainly this will be the last encounter between our species. We tried for a long time to preserve our home world, but we have no more than a sentimental attachment to it now, and it is definitely too dangerous to remain here."

"Because we humans use so much iron?" I hazarded.

"Oh no. Because of the planet's determination to blow itself up."

That seemed to make no sense whatever. I said so. He

eyed me speculatively for a while, and appeared to reach
a decision.

"We've tried very often to explain to you humans what
the danger is," he said. "Unfortunately your comprehen-
sion is so limited, you've treated our warnings as an absurd fiction. I wonder, though, whether someone as relatively well informed as you might not be equipped to
grasp the gist. It's worth trying . . . To begin with, tell
me what you know about the stars."

As you have often told me somewhat brusquely, Leo,
I'm no scientist! However, thanks to my acquaintance
with you some facts have rubbed off on me. I gave a summary account, as well as I could, of contemporary astron-
omy, and Toby was reasonably pleased.

"So you've finally discovered that the stars are emitting
information!" he exclaimed. "Indeed you seem to have
extracted quite a lot of knowledge from their spectra.
Good! Now you must realise that there is a genuine
analogy between the information which the stars are
broadcasting, and what we are doing now: talking. The
nature of both is determined by a more or less organised
series of events. To employ an image which you may con-
ceivably find helpful, the radiation of a star can be regarded as one continuous exuberant shout about what the
star is experiencing in its interior."

I said, "Are you trying to tell me that the stars are
conscious beings?"

With positively human sarcasm he said, "You have a
most apt word in your language: anthropomorphic! I did
not say, 'is,' I said, 'can be regarded as.' You are insuffi-
ciently evolved to come closer to the truth. Now, to continue: this planet we are on at the moment can be regarded (mark the way I express it!) as being envious of
the stars—jealous of their more vital and vivid experience."

I was going to interrupt again, but he prevented me with a stern gesture.

"In a never-ending attempt to experience events of a stellar nature, planets bring together masses of radio-active material. You have legends of my species as miners, haven't you?"

"Kobolds," I said feebly. "Gnomes. That's right."

"What would we need to mine for? Gold? We don't use money! Jewels? We don't wear ornaments! No, we were frustrating attempts by this planet to bring together sufficient radioactive mass to initiate a stellar reaction in its crust. Thanks to intervention by you humans, however, we have given up the struggle and decided to retire elsewhere."

"What are we supposed to have done?" I cried.

He ignored me. "It is far easier for the planet to assemble vast amounts of light, fusible elements in one place than to concentrate radioactives, since the latter tend to heat up, melt and dissipate without causing more than a few volcanic eruptions. But the light elements, such as those which power the stars, are stable, and can be accumulated in as large a quantity as necessary to await the initiating impulse."

Thanks to your own explanations, Leo, I did finally get the point. Duffer though I am where scientific matters are concerned, I followed perfectly your own account, which you gave me a few days ago—I mean, which you had given me a few days previously—concerning attempts to trigger a solar reaction in light elements without the cumbrous and dangerous employment of an atomic bomb. I recall you saying that the chief hope of accomplishing this resided in the properties of that device I barely understand, which they call a "laser." (Seven years having gone by, I suppose this is virtually ancient history to you; to me, however, it's only a week in the past.)

Nonetheless, my mind revolted at the proposition that

Mother Earth was capable of will and intention, like a living being. I said as much to Toby—I fear, more bluntly than was polite. I called the notion, candidly, rubbish!

He sighed. "I hardly expected you to be convinced verbally," he conceded. "I gave you the verbal explanation only in the hope that it would equip you to understand what you are going to experience now."

And with a leap like—like a hungry flea!—he jumped up at my chest and *stabbed* me.

The species from which Toby's kind descended must, I imagine, have been related to a type of wasp I've read about, which stings its prey into a state of suspended animation. (Is it an ichneumon? I have a hazy recollection . . .)

For, piecing together what I've learned since I woke up, I can only believe that as a result of this stab, no mark of which can be discerned, I passed into a miraculous coma. I must have been hidden by some extraordinary means, for when I awoke I was in the same cave, and I've established that the cave was searched when I was reported missing and my tent and other belongings were discovered, but not my unconscious self.

And—in my mind at any rate—I was taken into Fairyland.

Perhaps I'm the first human being to make sense of what I saw. Certainly I'm not the first human being to undergo that experience. I suspect that the hero of *The Rime of True Thomas* and suchlike other legends was so confused that the best he could make of the images and concepts overwhelming his mind was to convert them into everyday analogies: thus the splendour of the stars became the splendour of a fairy court, with magnificent kings and queens populating it.

I felt as though a few short hours were passing and in fact seven years and almost three months went by. During that time I saw and heard and felt (my senses were so to say "cross-connected") the literal truth of what Toby had been telling me. I heard the joyful communication of the stars—which, it strikes me in passing, may have been heard by others before me. The psalmist spoke of them "rejoicing before the Lord," did he not? And how about "the music of the spheres"?

More alarmingly, I sensed and perceived the dull, cloddish envy of the planets, including our own, and I saw how they plot and scheme to explode themselves so that they may—however briefly—experience stellar ecstasy.

Including our own, Leo!

When I awoke I was naked except for some damp half-rotted rags; moreover, of course, I was filthy and ravenously hungry. I stumbled into Dartleby and convinced the local GP, with much difficulty, that I was not an escaped madman. (He told me, by the way, that physically I'm in fine shape bar a hint of undernourishment.) But I did not, naturally, offer a full account of my experience to him. Unless I had imparted the details to someone, though, I realised I would never be able to sleep tonight, which is why I've set it out in letter form.

Since you have the misfortune to be the only nuclear physicist I know, I'm wholly and utterly dependent on you. So indeed are we all! I've no idea where these light, fusible elements are being concentrated, or even what the trigger is to be—a nuclear bomb-test, one of your lasers, an accident in a power plant . . .

But when the time comes (and believe me, what Toby showed me has convinced me that it *will* come), Earth is going to become with high delight a small though temporary star. And it's obvious what will happen to us.

So you've *got* to believe me, Leo. You *must*.

Yours ever—
(*signed* Barney)
Barnaby Gregg, QC.

THE INCEPTION OF THE EPOCH OF
MRS. BEDONEBYASYOUDID

New York, late on a cold Thursday evening in January: an all-night Chinese restaurant in the East Village; the observation platform of the Empire State Building; the underground garage of a large apartment block; the 125th Street station of the IRT.

The lady is in four places at the same time tonight. Not bad for a trial run. Next week, forty. The month after next perhaps four hundred. In the winter snow, the prints of her high-buttoned boots, the dragging scuff-marks of her long drab skirt, and here and there—apparently at random—the traces of her birch for naughty children.

The last recorded sign of her predecessor occurred two weeks ago in Tompkins Square. Two draft-resisters had set up a Christmas crib containing a picture of a baby flayed to death with napalm, and invited passers-by to sign a memorial book balanced on a music rack they had —ah—borrowed from the nearby bandstand. And there, in neat script, the ink running a little in pale blue tears as snowflakes melted down the page, was inscribed: "Do as you would be done by. Amen."

But that was last year, and the last entry in the book. This year . . .

"Ah, it's cold up there, man! And it's late—you'll only have a few minutes anyway!"

But the young whiteman wanted to go up, a dollar fifty worth of wanting: in his jacket with fur trimming at cuffs and collar, big clumsy boots but no gloves or hat. His ears were pink at their tips like neon signs on low current. So, sighing, the elevator operator took him up, the only person on the high platform overlooking the city, clutching a package under his left arm and mechanically moving his fingers to stop them going numb with cold.

Alone, he set his burden down on the surrounding ledge and looked over towards the wire nets preventive of suicide, brushing at snow settled since the last clearance job. He walked all around looking at the brilliance of the city, the gaudy lights, the high magnificent buildings. It was clear now, and going to freeze like hell. Earlier it had snowed.

Sure of being for a moment unobserved, the whiteman opened one end of his package and bestowed a kiss on the thing he took out of it. More tipped than thrown over the side, leaving barely a mark in the accumulated snow on the wire nets, it landed and lay where it had fallen.

Hating to expose himself to the touch of the cold, the elevator operator called last trip down. Obediently the young whiteman went, his breath misting before his mouth.

It was five minutes before Friday.

It was the real New Year's Eve.

"Now, let's see . . ." Quietly moving from car to car, the five dark figures checking and assessing Buicks and Cadillacs, Mercedes and Jaguars. "Right here is fourteen-oh-four's. He goes 'way down town. Wall Street somewhere, I guess."

In a smart uniform, white top of cap contrasting with ebony of face, white hands in gloves of course, the blackman tapped the dash because the fuel gauge sometimes stuck at zero. It swung over and showed three-quarters full.

"That one," said another of the group. A third, in a shabby mackinaw of dark blue and dark green tartan, dropped on his back and wriggled underneath, feeling in darkness for the gas-tank. The magnet in his hand snicked and he cursed, slid it loose against its powerful drag, and re-sited it. To the side which remained exposed he attached a flat can. The can held an acid-glass timer, not very accurate but good enough if the target zone was more than an hour wide, mercury fulminate, and ordinary powder extracted from shotgun shells. The fourth and fifth members of the group, sharing the load, were toting a cardboard carton containing similar cans, plus six specials employing a 1.5-volt dry cell and a timer adapted from a Japanese watch retailing around Forty-second Street for $8.95.

"And this one belongs to a cat in publishing. Goes up to the north end of Madison Avenue some place, far's I know."

"Great."

But its gas-tank was almost empty. Instead, they chose one belonging to an advertising copywriter working a block or two further south. And another, and another. There were seventy cars parked in the basement garage. They reserved the specials for owners who were likely to be on the move at 10 A.M. Friday.

When the carton was empty the blackman shook hands with his visitors and went back to the little office from which he kept watch and ward. Removing the .38 whose licence fee was charged against the management costs of the building from the drawer in which it lived, he sited it artistically on the floor, where it might be expected to have fallen when he was clubbed unconscious.

"Okay, man, hit me," he signed. "But aim careful,

huh? And when you get around to tying my legs for chrissake don't give me gangrene."

It was three-fifteen. The birchmarks had not yet appeared in the snow. Before they did, traffic would have muddled it into slush.

Candy, gum—products for orally fixated travellers hating to give up their cigarettes for even the length of a subway ride. On the walls stark as a public urinal's, big black figures: 125, 125, 125 . . .

Coming off a local and crossing the platform as though waiting for the late *late* show of an express to take him 'way *way* uptown, the brownman peered, this way, that. From the side pocket of a big hunching overcoat like a twenties college boy's, bootlegger size but not containing illicit whisky, he removed a thing in crumpled brown paper. No one else except a shivering bum whispering dreams of wine. At the back of the miniaturised market, consolation for a coin, the exactly designed contents of the paper package: it fitted, it wore a sleek red-paint overcoat of its own, shabbied by exposure while wet to the air of New York five storeys above the street. It looked as though it belonged where he had put it.

When the next train came by, bound far northward into the uncharted regions of the Bronx, the brownman boarded it and rode away to anywhere.

It was four thirty-five.

Stale cooking smells lingered in the air of the Celestial City (present incarnation) because the door was always slammed rapidly shut after every entrance by an alert little man with almond eyes. Too cold out to waste the cost of precious heat on the public thoroughfare . . .

At this time, though, only the wanderers ignorant of the presence of the lady. Down by the door end, leaning close across a table, a boy about nineteen, a girl much younger, holding hands and asking over and over for more jasmine tea (and the boy vanishing to the toilet because of it, three times for the girl's one), too desperate for each other's company to separate and go home, well dressed enough to justify going on with the supply and no doubt lacking a place to lie down together. This surrogate welcome. Also a very old man mumbling the rice he insisted on having overcooked, wetly sauced: detritus of the street.

Watching from the far back of the retaurant, sallow, self-contained, dark-suited: a man in his early thirties, short, lean, thoughtful of expression.

The door opened and a whiteman entered, sat down at a table some distance from the loving couple. When he had ordered food and tea and sampled them the watcher rose and courteously approached his table—as it were, "Is it good, sir?" Armoured by Asian anonymity, he waited for a reply to the question he had not uttered.

Chewing, the whiteman said, "Very cool. Both Hal and Eugene called in, said they had no trouble. And mine went pretty smooth."

A nod. An . . . *inscrutable* smile. It was 5:05 A.M. The lady's boots were printing the outside snow.

At exactly nine-seven, when the throat of Fifth Avenue was choked with traffic and snow, one of the daughter elements of a so-called pomegranate bomb—filched from the stores of a company responsible for supplying key munitions to the government of South Viet-Nam—exploded on the anti-suicide nets of the Empire State Building. Just one. Although the device had been designed for optimum effect following the ground-burst of a "mother" bomb containing two dozen such "daughters," the force of its explosion was adequate to rupture the wire netting it rested on and the small steel spheres it emitted caused a substantial number of casualties. There were no fatalities, but Gloria Schultz, eighteen, entered a permanent coma owing to severe brain-damage, while Stephen V. Lord, a cabdriver of forty-four, sustained lifetime loss of the use of his right arm when one penetrated the roof of his vehicle, and three-year-old twins Edward and Elvin Marshall, being taken by their mother Mrs. Sarah Marshall to see a pediatrician, were struck in the head and stomach respectively and sustained injuries entailing long-term hospitalisation. Additionally there were more than two hundred minor casualties reported to the city health authorities, some directly due to the steel balls, some to secondary effects such as flying glass from broken windows.

At nine-nine, during one of the busiest periods of the day at the 125th Street IRT station, a container began to leak a gas officially termed "DN," not recommended —to quote the army manual regarding its applicability —"where fatalities are impermissible." A panic ensued. Mrs. Gladys Kane, sixty-two, was trampled to death in front of the exit turnstiles. Broken arms and feet were treated at a nearby hospital and Vivian L. Borghardt, nineteen, lost an eye apparently as the result of being struck by an umbrella carried by Jane Prink, twenty-four, a fashion model. No deaths could be attributed directly to the gas, although three days later Dr. Harold W. Stranding, well-known expert on bronchial and pleural conditions, forecast that a number of patients who were afterwards to succumb to such proximate causes as pneumonia might have their demise accelerated by their exposure to the DN.

Between nine-twenty and ten-forty, thirty-six cars, subsequently established to have been parked overnight in the basement garage of an apartment block whose night attendant was at the time hospitalised with a suspected fracture of the skull, suffered explosions of their gas-tanks, occasioning twenty-eight direct and eleven indirect fatalities and a substantial number of severe burns to pedestrians walking past those of them which had been parked on the street when they blew up. A Buick belonging to Ralph S. High, thirty-five, sales representative for a chemical corporation, caught fire while travelling at the legal limit on a parkway in New Jersey en route to his employers' major factory and caused a pile-up of eight cars when it slewed across the road. Five of the eleven indirect fatalities resulted from this crash.

There were also two cases of paralysis from the waist down, and Mrs. Eleanora Gage, twenty-three, a wife of eight months, lost the baby she was expecting in early March.

Anonymous among the staff of a Chinese restaurant in the East Village—who, after all, can tell these Asiatics apart?—Ngo Duy Thinh listened critically as the news of "accident" after "accident" broke into the regular broadcasts of WNBC. He seldom bothered to glance up at the screen of the set. Certainly he did not display the enthusiasm with which his companions, a whiteman, a brownman and a blackman lingering over a late Chinese breakfast, greeted each new disaster as it was reported by the commentator. He had seen too many similar events—three dimensional, live and in colour—while serving as Chief of Casualty Administration with the National Liberation Front of South Viet-Nam, commonly called the Viet Cong . . . or "Charlie."

Yet, after years of one-sided suffering, it did not seem too soon for the reign of Mrs. Doasyouwouldbedoneby to give way to the epoch of Mrs. Bedonebyasyoudid.

He spoke up suddenly, conscious that his voice was rasping in his throat, conscious even more of the fact that his listeners were nominally the people who collectively had educated him in hate.

"All right!" (The words were foreign, alien, awkward,

but they had to be organised into sense.) "Now, those stone-scows working out of Pier Number Seventy-Two, the ones you suggested as platforms for mortars. Have we made any contact with the people operating them?"

"Trust you always to be thinking one step ahead," the whiteman said. "That's my boy!"

But I'm not. Haven't you—even you—learned that by now? It's been a hell of a long time.

Aloud, though, Ngo Duy Thinh merely repeated his question. It was not until twelve-twenty that the tanks of the United States Third Armoured Division began to clank and rumble down Houston Street at walking pace, flanked by men in helmets who carried carbines with full magazines.

THE OLDEST GLASS

The references invoked are to Ausonius, Epigrammata
LXV, *and the Arabic legend of Plato and Aristotle—
Aflatun and Aristu*

Mirrors have always been a threat to men
—and women, worse; you know how once for all
Lais renounced hers to the goddess. Water,
though, must be the oldest glass. Very long
before history the pattern was set:
some man stared down, and the same man stared back

—magic! His fear, which caused him to cringe back,
shamed his descendants. That is why some men
are hypnotised by oceans, and spend all
their lives fighting the terror of the water
which may show them themselves. They partly long
for, partly fear, that truth. Their course is set

for epochs where night, day, sunrise, sunset,
moon, stars, wind, seem more real. They travel back
along the common heritage of men . . .
which blunts the sting. It's said that out of all
those who have dared the mirror of the water
just two have looked into it bravely long.

That Greek port's quay was crowded right along
with sightseers, so absolutely set
on watching the departure, none looked back
at the arrival: two sick, shaggy men
aboard a rotten hulk, its rigging all
crusted with salt, riding low in the water.

Much had been done: provisions, wine, sweet water
were stored below. They had dreamed for so long
of this adventure. Both their hearts were set
on circling the globe and coming back.
(Their crew were less keen. Indeed, what sane men
would let philosophers command them all?)

They saw it, that sad hulk, and knew it all
must happen; on the mirror of the water
they saw themselves return after a long
voyage, grizzled and ancient. So they set
their sails for sea. All mirrors must give back
the truth. You may add nothing but "amen"
to this tale of two men who travelled all
the world-wide water, let their beards grow long,
and watched themselves set out as they came back.